MEET
THE CLIENTS
OF ARTHUR KIRKLAND:

The Black Transvestite in the Blonde Wig—he has a dream: the most beautiful dress in the world. And a nightmare: going to jail.

The Wealthy Man in Middle-age and in Sticky Situations—he has a fantasy: very young, very beautiful, and very bonde women. And he has a reality: a very real wife.

The Judge in Love with the Judgment Day—he has a problem: he eats his lunch on the ledge outside his window; he tries to shoot himself but can't reach the trigger; and he flies helicopters without any gas. And if he solves *his* problem, a lot of innocent people will have even bigger problems: because this judge has the gift of every great judge—compassion.

The Lawyer with the Guilty Client—he *had* a client: but he got him off on a legal technicality. Then he had a bit of news: his client just murdered someone else. Then he had himself fitted for a new jacket: a very straight one.

A JOE WIZAN PRESENTATION

A NORMAN JEWISON FILM

AL PACINO
". . . AND JUSTICE FOR ALL"
JACK WARDEN

JOHN FORSYTHE

and LEE STRASBERG

MUSIC BY DAVE GRUSIN

WRITTEN BY VALERIE CURTIN &
BARRY LEVINSON

EXECUTIVE PRODUCER JOE WIZAN

PRODUCED BY NORMAN JEWISON &
PATRICK J. PALMER

DIRECTED BY NORMAN JEWISON

A COLUMBIA PICTURES RELEASE

Columbia Pictures

"...AND JUSTICE FOR ALL"

a novel by Robert Grossbach

based on a motion picture written by
Valerie Curtin & Barry Levinson

BALLANTINE BOOKS · NEW YORK

Library of Congress Catalog Card Number: 79-52506

ISBN 0-345-28268-X

Manufactured in the United States of America

First Edition: October 1979

For Jeff Brown, who found me twice

The author appreciatively acknowledges Ira H. Leibowitz, Esq., who was kind enough to provide supplemental anecdotal and background material on the legal profession.

"...AND JUSTICE FOR ALL"

THE sleeping man next to him was urinating in his pants, but this was to be expected. It was not the first time Arthur Kirkland had been in jail, and he knew from experience that a certain number of runaway body functions were *de rigeur* for the inhabitants. People urinated, defecated, ejaculated, sneezed, and bled without warning, uncontrollably. *No big deal.* The dark stain spread slowly over the drunk's crotch and worked its way down the legs of his trousers. Nimbly, Arthur moved sideways on the concrete floor.

Funny, he thought, how quickly your levels of abstraction changed. Only hours earlier he'd been contemplating legal technicalities, trying to recall details of a 1954 ruling on bail by the Supreme Court. Now he sat idly, speculating on how soon pee would leak out from the pants cuff of the sleeping man next to him. The concrete pressed into the bottom of his spine.

He was a medium-height, dark-haired man with quick, penetrating eyes and full lips that had given him much anxiety as a youth. Fearful that they'd crossed the border from sensual to thick, he had often kept them sucked in part way and learned to live with the chapping. Time had redirected his attention. Thirty minutes ago he'd tried briefly to sleep, tried to convince himself that the hard surface would work orthopedic miracles on his back, that lying on the floor of a lock-up was really a healthful pursuit, the jail a spa for the lawless—but, of course, it hadn't worked. How could anyone sleep amid the noises, the movement, the people, the crowded quarters?

Arthur's own cell held five men; the adjacent one held four. The two on the other side of the corridor held three and five respectively. It didn't take long—a few hours in jail and you were an accomplished counter. Aside from attending to bodily necessities and abusing your comrades, what else was there to do? He looked around at the odd assortment of sleeping, disheveled humanity: edgy, twitching addicts; confused teen muggers; flashers, people caught doing unnatural things in movie theaters; pimps in furs and broad brims; clean-cut gay hustlers; innocent men who seemed suspicious; numbers runners, men who'd gone through stop signs—the broken driftwood of luckless humanity swept up in the nets of the night. Except for Arthur and two others, all were black or Hispanic.

A noise outside the cell block intruded on his thoughts. The door pushed open and two policemen bustled in, shoving a black man ahead of them. The man wore a pale-blue dress and a blond wig that sat slightly askew on his narrow head. Orange lipstick had smeared down to his chin. He kept a pace ahead of the policemen as they walked, minimizing the pressure of their prodding fingers, maintaining an erect posture, as if this would assure his dignity. The whole cell-block came to life as the procession moved down the corridor.

"Man," said one of the pimps next to Arthur, "don't put that in here. She not my type."

"Hey," a brutish-looking fellow called from two cells over, "that's my wife you talkin' 'bout. She here for our con-ju-gal visit." He pressed his broad face against the bars. "C'mon, honey," he cooed to the transvestite. "Over here, sugar plum. Let daddy show you what he's got in his pants for you."

A Cuban in the cell across from Arthur raised his voice contemptuously. "Shit, she got the same thin' under her skirt thah you got in your pants."

2

"Hey," called out an effeminate black man, "you a natural blond?"

A low rumble of laughter echoed in the cell-block; even the police guards chuckled.

"Come on," continued the man, "you Clairol or you natural? You wanna show us a little? You got anything that's natural there?"

The policemen stopped the transvestite in front of one of the cells. The men inside crowded near the door, hooting and moaning derisively.

"Whoo, Chicken Delight! He deliver!"

"Man, gonna mix your peanut butter, baby. Gonna get me some round eye tonight!"

The transvestite jerked backward, but one of the policemen blocked his path. The other stepped forward and unlocked the cell door. "We got a lady here," said the officer loudly. "I thought you assholes were gentlemen." He pulled the prisoner into the cell and stood him up against the bars. "Okay, Agee, you got any concealed weapons they didn't catch up front?"

Arthur had risen and, like everyone else, was watching intently. He felt a curious mixture of outrage, pity, and disgust. Situations like this were always pathetic.

"He got somethin' concealed," the effeminate man called out, "but it ain't no weapon!"

Agee, pinned against the bars, was shaking his wig-covered head from side to side. His eyes were tightly shut.

"C'mon, kid," said the guard, beefy forearm pressuring Agee's neck, "you hiding anything we should know about? You got a nail file up your ass, maybe? Hairpins?"

Tears of laughter streamed down the Cuban's face.

Agee moaned involuntarily.

"Whaddaya say you strip down just to make sure," continued the guard.

A round of spontaneous applause came from the prisoners. Agee twisted his head and looked at the

3

jeering inmates, then turned imploringly to the guard. "Please," he whispered. "No. Please."

The other policeman grinned. "Off with the clothes," he barked belligerently.

Agee began to sway and the first policeman held him upright. Agee reached to remove the wig. "Leave the wig on," ordered the guard.

Show time, thought Arthur, as Agee slowly started to unbutton his dress. There was no denying it, the urge to watch someone being humiliated was primal. His cellmates were crowded against the bars, eyes transfixed. The words *horrible fascination* came to Arthur's mind. That's the way people witnessed all sorts of primitive, savage, debasing behavior in cheap detective novels and murder stories. A seductive mixture of identity and revulsion, a fusion of the human and bestial. Arthur turned away, moved slowly toward the back of the cell. To give in to those impulses meant to be diminished as a man; it was important to resist. He passed the two derelicts still asleep on the floor and sat down facing the rear wall. He tilted his head back and stared at the ceiling, listening as the sounds of whistling and clapping increased.

Agee was left in only a pair of pink nylon panties and the blond wig.

"Take off the pants," said the guard.

Agee began to shiver. "Please. I don't want to."

"You want someone to help you?"

A half-dozen offers of assistance were immediately audible among the prisoners. Agee whimpered.

The cell-block door opened and another policeman entered. He walked down the corridor, nodded a quick hello to the guards holding Agee, glanced peremptorily at the near-naked man, then continued on to the cell that held Arthur. He unlocked the door.

Arthur turned and stood up.

"Let's go," said the policeman.

Arthur nodded silently, followed the officer out of

4

the cell, and waited while the man locked the door behind them. They walked toward the cell-block entrance, passing Agee, who by this time was naked, his legs spread apart. The other prisoners were calling out taunts as the guards grinned.

"Show her to the ladies' room."

"Shit, that ain't no lady."

"Sure comes close, though. That looks to me to be no more than an inch of dangling fury."

Arthur went through the cell-block door, carefully averting his eyes from Agee's beseeching stare.

Carl Bennett sat in the demolished Cadillac, head bent to clear the collapsed roof, and gazed, as he spoke, at the pieces of utility pole that had sheared off from the impact. Even crushed, he was impressive on the phone. Next to him, a woman in black watched a trickle of blood ooze from just above his eyebrow. She was having vague, garish fantasies of being Jackie Kennedy seated near a just-shot John, but balked at the part where she had to cradle him in her arms. The outfit she wore was simply too gorgeous to risk staining.

Bennett shouted into the phone. "What do you mean he— Where the hell is he?"

A silky woman's voice spoke from the other end. "He's in jail, sir."

"He's where?"

"In jail, Mr. Bennett."

Bennett, normally executive-quick on the uptake, seemed stunned. He pressed a monogrammed handkerchief to the cut on his forehead. "My lawyer's in jail?" he said incredulously.

"Yes, sir. Nothing big, contempt of court."

Bennett pinched his lips together. "He's too goddamn emotional. One of these days he'll be in real trouble. Anyway, get him. I've had a car accident."

"A car ac— Well, are you all right, sir?"

5

"Yes, yes, fine. A little head smash, that's all. I'm fine."

"Mr. Bennett, you really shouldn't have left the scene of the accident. If you weren't seriously—"

"Left?" said Bennett. "Who left? I'm in it!" He swiveled. Outside, two firemen were working with crowbars on the door of the Cadillac. The car had ended up on the sidewalk, just downwind of a dog obedience school and a Thom McAn shoe store. Bennett had an excellent view of a brick wall. "Can't you hear the confusion around me? You hear this noise? It's firemen trying to get me out."

"You mean you're *in* the car?" said the voice, less silky now. "Calling from *in* the car?"

"I am trapped!" shouted Bennett. "Trapped because some half-assed son of a bitch—"

"Mr. Bennett, just calm down."

"Calm d— You calm down! I'm bent double, with glass covering me like sequins. I need a lawyer!"

"I'll try to get hold of Arthur just as soon as they release him, Mr. Bennett."

"What? I can't— Hold it." Bennett placed the receiver on the dashboard. He looked out at the firemen. "Fellas . . . hey, guys . . . hey, hold it, guys!"

One of the firemen peered back in.

"Can't you see I'm on the phone?" said Bennett. "Keep it down, for chrissake. I can't hear myself think."

The officer placed a large Manila envelope on the desk and shoved it gingerly in Arthur's direction. Arthur tore it open and emptied the contents as the officer checked off the items on a clipboard: wallet containing eight dollars cash, no credit cards; key case with fourteen keys; miscellaneous bits of scrap paper with cryptic notes; five tissues; Timex watch, fully wound, but stopped. Arthur began counting the money.

"Understand you almost punched Judge Fleming,"

said the officer, chuckling. "Any reason in particular?"

"Mathews," said Arthur, "why don't you get that kid out of there and put him someplace else?"

The officer shrugged. "They're just having some fun with him."

"Yeah, fun. You guys have a great sense of humor. You wouldn't find it so amusing from the other side of the bars."

"Some of the guys get bored. This is a boring job, Arthur. You gotta take your fun where you find it. You gotta learn to appreciate the little foibles and deviations of humanity. To you, it's still new and exciting 'cause you only been here two, three times."

Arthur placed his wallet in his back pocket and began gathering up the scraps of paper. "Believe me," he said, "it's not new and exciting. It's repulsive."

"You better ease up on the judge," said Mathews.

Arthur slipped on his watch, checked it against the wall clock. "He's your kind of guy, huh?" He reset the time. Actually, the watch rarely worked. Arthur reset it ten times a day, but somehow could never bring himself to get a new one.

"Yeah, he's a tough man," said Mathews. He looked at Arthur sharply. "Hates scum as much as we do."

Arthur gathered his keys and tissues and headed toward the door. He smiled at Mathews. "Nice," he said. "Glad you found a friend."

Outside, he found a pay phone and dialed the office. "It's me," he said. "I'm out. Anything doing?"

He listened as the secretary told him.

Bennett was having visions of paleontology: he would be trapped in the car forever, unable to be freed; a mud slide would bury him and the woman, and a million years later, teams of hairless, toeless men would dig them up intact, imagining, perhaps, that the car was part of his body. They were surrounded now by police redirecting traffic, firemen washing oil and gasoline off the street, curious spectators craning their necks to get a better view. (The newspapers always referred to *crowds of gaping onlookers,* but Bennett could not see anyone gaping. Actually, he hadn't seen anyone gape in years.) The woman next to him had long since abandoned her Jackie fantasy and was concentrating now on not panicking. Bennett puffed out his cheeks just as a BMW sedan squealed around a corner and pulled up to the curb. Arthur got out quickly, still wearing the same rumpled suit he'd had on in prison. He stepped around two firemen, approached the crumpled Cadillac, and looked in at Bennett.

"You all right?"

Bennett stared out sullenly. "I'm wonderful. I just decided to stop here and rest in this position for three or four hours." He shook his head. "Meet any hardened criminals you liked?"

"I gather you're okay, then," said Arthur.

"Yes, gather that. I just thank God I've got a big car instead of one of those economy numbers. Saving gas does you no good when you're dead."

"Call the EPA," said Arthur. "They'll want to hear about that."

Bennett's face tightened. "I want you to sue the son of a bitch who did this to me. Nail him good. Every cent he's got."

There was a brief squeal of rending metal and suddenly the door on the opposite side was wedged open. The firemen helped the woman out first, and then Bennett slid over and squeezed through the gap. "The days of svelteness are gone," he muttered, as he brushed off his trousers. He leaned over the top of the car. "Every nickel, Arthur, you hear?"

But Arthur was already walking around the accordioned hood, and Bennett had to turn to face him. "Don't even leave him enough for carfare," he continued. "He shouldn't be able to afford to buy his

8

wife a pair of bloomers—which reminds me . . ." He looked at the woman, who stood nearby. "You okay?"

She shrugged.

"Disappear," said Bennett.

The woman began to move away.

"Thank God," said Bennett, turning back to Arthur, "thank God I can walk." Just then his legs buckled and Arthur grabbed him as he teetered unsteadily.

"Better change that to thank God you can wobble," said Arthur.

Bennett lowered his voice. "She wasn't hurt, so nothing in the report, okay? Okay?"

"Yeah."

"No need for the wife to know, right?"

"Right. Don't worry about it."

Two ambulance attendants wheeled a gurney over and Bennett sat down. "After all," he said, "I was your first. You know, Arthur? I was your first client. You broke cherry on me."

Arthur remembered; it was not that long ago. Ten years actually. He'd been out of law school for five years, had clerked for three. He'd had a watch that worked then, and he'd still had his illusions. . . . "Carl, this is not the time to go down nostalgia lane, here. Go to the hospital. Get checked out."

"Would you lie back, sir?" said one of the ambulance attendants to Bennett.

Bennett didn't listen. "You're the best, Arthur. I thought so then, and I still think so. Get every nickel. Then have him put away."

"I'll make sure he gets the death penalty," said Arthur.

"Lie back, sir," repeated the attendant. He put two fingers on Bennett's chest and Bennett gently folded down and backward.

"Death is okay, too," said Bennett.

Arthur patted him on the shoulder. Lying there, some of the ferocity had diminished. Arthur could almost forget that Bennett was one of the most power-

9

ful big businessmen in the Western hemisphere, certainly in Baltimore—and see him as a bent and folded accident victim. A man being taken away. A man whose car had been turned to scrap. "You take care," said Arthur.

"Jesus," said Bennett, "you stink! Someone piss on you?"

"Not quite," said Arthur, his new image of Bennett beginning to fade. "I was too fast for him."

"You also look like shit," said Bennett.

The image was gone. "Get him out of here," said Arthur to the attendants.

They began to wheel Bennett toward the waiting ambulance. Arthur walked alongside.

"Make sure no one uses my car phone," said Bennett, ignoring him. "I'm in the hospital, some jerk could call Rome."

"Accidents seem to bring out the best in your nature."

They were almost to the ambulance doors when Bennett spotted the man who'd been driving the other car. He was short and wore wire-rimmed spectacles and stood near one fender clutching the antenna mast. Actually, very little else was left of his car but the fender and antenna. The trunk had been pushed into the rear seat, and the engine somehow ended up near the steering wheel.

"You son of a bitch!" yelled Bennett, jumping up from the gurney. "You Nazi homo Commie mother creep! You maniac!"

The small man dazedly raised his head. "Look at my car," he said quietly. "You wrecked it. It's all gone now. Totaled."

"*I wrecked it?*" screamed Bennett. "*Me?*" He rolled his eyes. "You Neanderthal lunatic. You! You did it! You!"

Arthur grabbed Bennett around the shoulders. "You want a stroke or something? Calm down!"

Bennett ignored him, kept struggling.

"Get him to relax," said Arthur to the ambulance attendants. "Give him something."

One of the attendants hooked a forearm around Bennett's neck.

"You'll have to deal with my lawyer!" yelled Bennett, perspiring now, his face flushed.

The other driver had turned away, however, and was talking to no one. "Thirty-five more payments," he said softly. "Thirty-five."

"The death penalty!" ranted Bennett from the moving gurney. "You'll die for this!" He pointed up to Arthur. "You see this man? This is the best there is. You lost before you started. The man is a shark."

Bennett had again begun to rise, and Arthur helped one of the attendants hold him down. "Carl, I'm not a shark," he whispered.

"I want the jugular on this one," said Bennett. "No compromises, no prisoners."

"Carl," said Arthur wearily, "take a nap."

Bennett lay back. "I've got a terrible headache."

"It'll be all right," reassured Arthur. He watched as Bennett was lifted into the ambulance and the doors shut behind him. Like a mad dog, he thought, snapping to the end. "Don't worry," he shouted to the departing vehicle, "I'll take care of everything."

The sirens began to wail, and the revolving light started its spin. Arthur looked over at the other driver, still clinging to the remnant of his car.

"Thirty-five payments to go," repeated the man, as if in explanation of the clinging. "I was thrown clear."

Arthur walked over to a policeman. "Isn't there someone to take care of him? He needs help."

"I don't know," said the cop. "He insisted he wasn't injured. Said so himself." He looked down at Arthur. "You a relative or something?"

"Me?" said Arthur. "No. I'm nobody." He walked over to the other driver.

"What am I gonna do?" asked the man.

"Come on," said Arthur, "I'll take you over to the hospital."

"I'm all right."

"Yeah, yeah, I know, but come on anyway." He put his hand on the man's shoulder. Come on, they'll just take a look at you, that's all. What've you got to lose?"

The man seemed uncertain.

"Come on."

"Oh, God," said the man, "I can't afford all this." He put a hand to his face. Tears ran from under his spectacles and out between his fingers.

Supporting the man under the arms, Arthur led him toward his car. "Look, you're alive," he said. "And you're not badly hurt. Be thankful for that at least. At least you have your life."

"Not me," said the man. "The other guy. He has my life."

Arthur helped him into the car, then crossed to the driver's side and turned the key in the ignition. The man was staring glazedly out the windshield. "Listen," said Arthur, after a moment, "you didn't hear this from me, but why don't you call Norman Reed. He's in the book, Charles Center. He'll take care of you, and he's fair."

The man said nothing, gave no sign that he'd heard.

Arthur headed for the hospital.

2

ARTHUR parked on Fayette Street and walked the two blocks to the municipal courthouse. It was late autumn, and the sky was a smothering, flattened blanket of gray; a chilly dampness wafted inland from the harbor. Arthur hugged his jacket around him as he climbed the steps. Hurriedly, he moved through the marbled hallway, passing groups of lawyers and clients as he walked. He had observed this scene nearly every day for the past ten years. The late morning courtroom breaks, the strategy talks, last minute details, the desperate inhalation of cigarette smoke, calming of bewildered relatives, the gossip, the deals —it never changed. He caught snatches of conversation.

". . . best bet is to request a postponement," a lawyer was saying. "This would put us into late January. . . ."

". . . and say 'Yes, sir' when the judge asks you a question," insisted a mother to a pimpled teen-ager. "And look at him when he talks to you. George? George, you hear? I said . . ."

". . . DA's office is willing to go for two years, and one year probation."

"That's a lotta fuckin' time, man."

"Then let's hold off. See what they've got behind door number two."

Arthur walked on, passing Big Mitch Danowski and Herman Holowitz when he turned a corner. Holo-

13

witz's stomach spilled over his trouser tops as he attempted to simulate a tennis stroke.

"No good," said Big Mitch, whose specialty was intimidation. "You're bending it at the wrist."

Dark-bearded, intense, finger-pointing, he could sometimes even get judges to back off. He turned as he saw Arthur. "Hey, Art. How ya doin'?"

"Good," said Arthur pleasantly.

"You mean 'well,' " corrected Big Mitch. Then, returning to Holowitz, "Give me the racquet."

Holowitz handed over the imaginary racquet.

"You hold it like this," said Big Mitch, demonstrating. "And you follow through like this. You get it?"

Arthur spotted Jay Porter, his law partner, down near the end of the corridor. Porter, a tall, thin, hyperactive type, was talking to Robert Wenke, one of their clients. Wenke was one of Baltimore's foremost young punks.

"I ain't kissin' nobody's ass," Arthur heard Wenke comment.

"I'm not asking you to kiss it," said Jay, calmingly. "Just give it a little pat. Or blow on it." He spotted Arthur. "Hey, Art! Hold on a second!"

Arthur stopped.

"I'll see you in the courtroom," Jay said to Wenke. "Don't, uh, you know, wander off." He left Wenke and moved toward Arthur.

"Hi ya, Jay."

Jay stopped three feet away. "Jesus, you really look like shit."

"That's the second time I've heard that in an hour," said Arthur. "Jail has a way of doing that to a guy."

"Why didn't you go home and change first?" said Jay.

"Hey, gimme a break," said Arthur. "I know the way I look, the way I smell, so . . . okay?"

Jay shrugged. "I'm just concerned, that's all. I've got a right to be concerned. What if *I* showed up in court like that? What would you think?"

Arthur paused. Jay Porter was a good man. They'd met nine years ago when Jay was representing one member of a burglary team and Arthur the other. Arthur remembered the first time he'd seen Jay's office—the shredded carpeting, the furniture spewing springs and stuffing, open law books on the chairs and floor—and then there was the desk. Arthur's jaw had literally fallen open. Atop the desk was a vast sea of papers, a shifting, tangled, enmeshed heap of yellow and white. Infinities were suggested—leaf piles from redwood forests, grains of sand. . . . Porter had seen his face. "Don't be misled," he had said quickly. "I know where everything is."

It was a lie. He couldn't find anything. His work was never ready on time. He got constant dunning notices from bill collectors. He was four months behind on his rent. His clients rarely paid him because he neglected to bill them. Arthur had liked him immediately.

The fact was that, despite his chaotic and overwhelming sloppiness, Jay Porter was a good lawyer. he cared passionately about the people he represented. His memory was so uncannily accurate (by necessity) that he remembered everything he could not find. He had a good working relationship with nearly every assistant DA in Baltimore and was well respected by judges. He knew the law, had, in fact, been fifth in his class at Georgetown University. And, paradoxically, he was a neat personal dresser with immaculate habits.

A year after they met, they teamed up. Arthur had helped Jay with organization and a filing system. Jay acted to restrain Arthur's temper and to wrench him out of long periods of depression and brooding. Jay's desk was still buried under paper but the thickness was now less than a foot. He once showed Arthur a hat he'd knitted. (Knitting was Jay's hobby.) The hat was an amorphous blob with many missed stitches, but

Arthur had bestowed numerous compliments. Shortly thereafter Jay made the mistake of placing it on his desk and the hat became just another bit of the rubble. Arthur had never seen it again.

He smiled now as Jay stood in the corridor. "Did I tell you, Jay, that you look very beautiful today? The blue ... it brings out your eyes."

Jay shook his head and trailed behind as Arthur turned for the men's room. Inside, Arthur bent over a sink while Jay laid his briefcase up against one of the urinals.

"I don't want to keep harping ..." said Jay.

"Then don't." Arthur splashed water on his face.

"... but with the Ethics Committee checking on everyone, you've got to watch it."

"Okay, I'll watch it."

"It's not something to be flip about."

"I'm not flip."

"Last week, two lawyers were disbarred on very minor charges ..."

"Selling two kilos of smack is not that minor, Jay."

"... and you're running around getting sent to jail on contempt. And it wasn't heroin, it was hashish."

"Look," said Arthur, wiping the back of his neck with a wet paper towel, "Fleming gets on my nerves."

"I don't care. You keep pushing him on that McCullaugh thing and there's going to be trouble. I'm telling you."

"McCullaugh's innocent and I can't get Fleming to reopen the case. It's driving me nuts."

Jay nodded. "I can understand that. You know I'm the last person to ever suggest abandoning a client. But there are times to fight and times to run."

Arthur reached for another paper towel to dry himself, but came up empty. "Fuck!" he said. He wiped his hands on his jacket, ran his sleeve over his neck.

Jay bent over his briefcase and removed a small bottle of cologne. "Here, put some of this on."

16

"Only you, Jay."

"Come on," said Jay.

Arthur took the bottle and splashed on some of the contents.

"Don't drown yourself, for chrissake," said Jay.

"I see. A little goes a long way. I'll think of you as I gag on this stuff all day."

"And I'll think of you whenever I bend over these urinals," said Jay, replacing the cologne in his brief-case. "By the way, I've got Fleming this morning, speak of the devil."

"Give him my love," said Arthur. He walked over to Jay and smoothed his collar. "Seriously, the blue . . . it's nice."

"Yeah," said Jay, "it's Fleming's favorite color."

There were only six people in the spectators' section, and three of them were reading newspapers. Jay and Robert Wenke sat at the defense table; Fleming, in the leather judge's seat behind the bench, loomed over them. He was a dignified-looking man in his mid-fifties with aquiline features set off by neatly trimmed silver hair. He gazed down at a file folder as he spoke.

"Mr. Wenke, how many times have you been before the bench?"

Wenke sneered. "Three times, Your Honor."

Fleming continued studying the file. "Yes, I see. One time for assault, once for arson, once for grand theft." He looked up. "And now we have child molestation." Fleming stared at the defendant. "What's the matter, Mr. Wenke? Can't you decide what you want to be when you grow up?"

Wenke grinned contemptuously.

"Is there *any*thing you want to say?" persisted Fleming.

"Yes, Your Honor, there is," said Wenke. "I am a loyal Colts fan."

Fleming nodded. "You are also a revolting, despicable scum of the earth who should be taken out and squashed like a cockroach."

Jay quickly sprang to his feet. "Judge Fleming, I object! My client has not been found guilty yet!"

Fleming looked at him derisively, and Jay wilted. It had been hopeless from the beginning. Arthur had not even wanted them to take the case, but Wenke's mother happened to be a friend of Jay's aunt Caroline, who had lent him five thousand dollars so he could finish law school. It was impossible to refuse. "She's a desperate woman," Aunt Caroline had argued, referring to Mrs. Wenke. "She raised Robert all by herself, and now there's no one who will take the case."

"Of course not," Jay had said. "The kid is rotten to the core. He's guilty."

"It's either you or the public defender."

"Let him go to Legal Aid."

"I've known the woman twenty-five years, Jay. Please, do it for me. Forget him. I would consider it a personal favor."

He took the case. Wenke had been selling dope to high school kids, then had worked his way down to junior high and, finally, elementary school. Enticing her with the promise of a marijuana cigarette, he had lured a fourth-grade girl to a vacant lot behind the school, lifted her dress, fondled her while she whimpered in terror, and then fled. A week later, for whatever reason, he'd loitered near the school again, was spotted by the girl, picked up, and arrested.

Fleming had called the calendar, and both Jay and Gilman, the assistant DA on the case, said they were ready. There were three charges against Wenke: possession of an illegal substance with intent to sell, corrupting the morals of a minor, and child molestation. "Take one for three," Fleming had instructed Gilman. He was asking that only one of the charges be prosecuted, a time- and cost-saving device. The assistant

DA readily agreed and chose the molestation charge. Later, Jay had tried to cop a plea without success. "Not on this one," Gilman had said, "and not with this kid."

It had been a minor achievement to even waive a trial by jury. Wenke refused to plead guilty ("I'm already a two-time loser") and refused to plead insanity ("I'll kill you if you claim I'm nuts"). As evidence, the little girl had a marijuana cigarette with Wenke's fingerprints on it ("I can't believe you gave her the joint," Jay had said, "if all you wanted was to molest her") and had returned to her house with torn panties and bruised thighs. A jury would probably have hung Wenke right there in the courtroom, but when Jay pointed out that he would have to put the girl on the stand and question her credibility, Fleming had agreed to hear the case in chambers.

There was little to use for defense. Two psychiatrists testified that Wenke was "sane, but dangerous." Wenke's mother appeared as a character witness ("He was a good boy"). Jay had briefly confused the little girl (he felt like a slime) but could not produce any real inconsistency in her story. Her identification of Wenke was unswerving.

In the courtroom, Judge Fleming looked at the clock. "Your objection is irrelevant, Mr. Porter. It is now nine-forty. At nine-forty-one he *will* be *guilty*."

Jay glanced at Gilman, sitting at the prosecution table ten feet away. Gilman shrugged.

"Will the defendant please rise," said Fleming.

In front of the bench, the bailiff snapped to attention. Slowly, with prodding from Jay, Wenke stood up.

The minute hand on the clock moved a tiny fraction of an inch.

"I find the defendant, Robert Wenke, guilty as charged," intoned Fleming. "Sentence to be passed at a later date."

He rapped the gavel as Wenke smirked.

Judge Rayford, a rugged ex-Marine, was caught up in a Gothic novel of passion and suspense. He had read it all through his breakfast of Melba toast and cottage cheese, all through his hour-long session on the toilet, and had even sneaked glances during court. After all, the fate of Loretta Swinbourne, heroine of *Love's Strange Passages,* was much more exciting than what became of some drug addict. In his chambers Judge Rayford read hungrily, tearing through the pages while munching on diet Fritos. Until he finished chapter fifteen, where Loretta discovers a secret room in her new husband's forbidding apartment, Courtroom D would remain in recess.

Arthur tilted his chair backward so that it leaned against the railing of the spectators' section. Next to him, Billy Gibson, his thin-faced, curly-haired, guilty client, drummed nervously on the defense table. Arthur heard a voice in his ear.

"You know that big yellow house down on Smith Avenue?"

Arthur glanced around, although he didn't have to. He could tell by the overpowering aroma of cologne that it was Warren Fresnell, obese and shrewd Keeper of Bad Taste for the Maryland Bar Association.

"Guess how much that cost on today's market?" continued Fresnell. Fresnell was a specialist in blown-up medical malpractice claims.

"I don't know," said Arthur.

"Take a guess."

Fresnell leaned over, the jacket of his maroon polyester leisure suit brushing the railing. He was overflowing with unnatural good cheer.

"Seven million," said Arthur.

"Come on, Art, be serious."

"Six million."

Next to Arthur, Billy Gibson stood up and stretched.

"Wrong," said Fresnell. "Two hundred and forty-

20

three thousand. That's some nut I got, huh?" He chuckled. "That's okay, you think I'm worried?"

"Yes," said Arthur.

"Wrong again. All I need are a couple of decent postoperative infections, a botched kidney, and I'm sailing in the clear. Give me an unnecessary mastectomy, and you make my year."

Billy Gibson had ambled several yards away.

"Tell ya something," said Fresnell, "your old house, the one you lost in your divorce settlement . . ."

"Don't say it," said Arthur.

"Do you know how much it would be worth now?"

"No."

"Take a guess."

"Seven million," said Arthur. In his mind, a fantasy was playing. Fresnell, dying from heart disease, is brought to the hospital for a last-chance operation that can be done by only one man in the country. On the operating table Fresnell looks up, discovers that the surgeon is someone he nearly ruined years before in one of his phony suits. Just as he goes under the anaesthetic, he hears the surgeon say, *"Now* I remember where I know you from. . . ."

Near the back of the courtroom, Don Keene, an assistant DA, was talking in low tones to an attractive young woman.

"Up to you, Don," said the woman.

"Then I say we go," said Keene. "The recess has got to be over in a few minutes and all I have left on the morning calendar is this illegal lottery case."

"Which means what?"

"Which means I'll be out of here by eleven-thirty."

The woman stared vacantly over his left shoulder.

The assistant DA leaned closer. "If you want, we can grab a little lunch first. Or anything else you want to grab. What do you say?"

The woman shrugged. "Fine. Did you know there's a guy eating something off your table?"

"Hmmm?"

"I think that guy is eating your evidence."

Engrossed, Keene did not understand. "Wha? Look, can't you—"

"That guy. The one you're prosecuting. He's eating the lottery tickets."

Keene pivoted sluggishly. At the front of the courtroom, Gibson was quietly cramming lottery tickets into his mouth, chewing, and swallowing methodically.

"Holy shit," said Keene softly. He raced down the aisle. "Hey!" he yelled. "Hey you, hold it!"

Gibson, seeing Keene approach, jammed a final fistful of tickets into his mouth and chewed furiously.

Keene got to the railing and vaulted over the gate. "Hey, you can't—" He grabbed Gibson around the throat, feeling the bobbing Adam's apple pressing against his forearm, his hard-won evidence beginning its peristaltic journey. "Son of a bitch!" he screamed.

Gibson failed to answer.

"Spit it out!" insisted Keene. "Spit it, or I'll—"

The two men fell backward to the floor as Arthur, hearing the commotion, stood up. For a moment, confused, he glanced at Fresnell. "What the hell's going on?"

Fresnell grinned. "You don't know?"

"No."

Keene had rolled over on top of Gibson and was trying to pry his mouth open.

"Your defendant's been noshing on the lottery tickets," said Fresnell.

Arthur walked slowly toward the grappling men.

"I thought it was a tactic," called Fresnell after him. "I thought you knew."

"Oh, terrific," said Arthur. He tapped Keene on the shoulder. "You're on my client," he said.

Keene was busily squeezing Gibson's cheeks. "I'm warning you—" he yelled, red-faced.

"Get the hell off him!" said Arthur.

"You can't win!" said Keene. A whitish pulp oozed out Gibson's mouth.

Arthur grabbed Keene's jacket collar and yanked backward as the assistant DA began pounding Gibson's head on the floor.

"We'll tear out your insides, you creep," ranted Keene. "We'll find them!"

"Are you crazy!" yelled Arthur. "You'll kill him!" He and Keene spilled onto the floor as Gibson made elaborate choking sounds.

"Don't swallow, you son of a bitch!" screamed Keene, clawing back toward the half-asphyxiated Gibson.

With Arthur hanging on his waist like a football defensive safety clinging to a fullback, Keene somehow made it to Gibson's end zone. By this time the bailiff and two court officers were also in the struggle, none of them really cognizant of the issues. The screaming, cursing men flopped uncontrollably in front of the witness stand.

In his chambers, Judge Rayford was coming to the end of the chapter. Her heart pounding, Loretta, the heroine, grasped the handle of the door to the hidden room, the door her scarred but handsome husband warned her she must never open. She pulled the handle toward her, looked in—and gasped.

The judge placed the bookmark neatly between the pages and closed the covers. He stood up, stretched, and glanced at the clock. Damn! It would be over an hour before he could get back to the story. He smoothed his robes, blew his nose, and stood up. As he walked down the little hall and paused at the door to the courtroom, he thought briefly of Loretta. What if he should find the same thing she did? He turned the doorknob.

Inside, a writhing mass of lawyers, policemen, and defendants struggled inconclusively in front of the bench. Rayford watched them calmly for several seconds, then reached deliberately beneath his robes. The .38 caliber pistol he pulled out had formerly been owned by the president of a garbage-hauling company. Rayford aimed carefully at the ceiling, and fired.

Outside the courtroom, fifty feet down the corridor, two policemen looked up from their conversation.

"Trouble," said the younger.

But the older one, following the direction of the sound, shook his head. "Courtroom D," he said. "It's Rayford, that's all."

Rayford stood with his smoking weapon. The fighting had come to a halt. "Gentlemen," Rayford said calmly, "need I remind you that you are in a court of law?"

3

IMMEDIATELY after the Gibson adjournment, Arthur raced to a small room on the third floor of the courthouse. A desk sergeant sat staring at a pile of papers as Arthur came in.

"Uh, 'scuse me."

The officer looked up. "Oh, Mr. Kirkland, well, what can we . . ."

"I want to see McCullaugh. Is he still here?"

The sergeant pursed his lips. "Yeah, I think . . . I dunno. They're getting ready to send him back."

"Where can I find him?"

"Check downstairs with loading."

Arthur nodded and left. Three minutes later he was outside, at the rear of the courthouse, as a group of manacled prisoners waited lined up near one wall. Arthur approached one of the guards, who was leaning against the waiting van.

"You have my client here. McCullaugh. Mind if I see him for a second?"

The guard, who'd been studying a clipboard, looked up. "Sure."

Arthur walked over to McCullaugh, a frail young man who seemed out of place next to the other prisoners. A second guard watched them closely as Arthur motioned McCullaugh to take a few steps away.

"Man," said McCullaugh, "you looked wiped out."

Arthur ignored him. "Listen, Jeff, I just want to reaffirm what I said to you yesterday." Arthur studied the young man's eyes, saw the soft, liquid centers.

"About what?"

"We're going to get you out. I promise you."

"I know," said McCullaugh, his voice quavering. "I know you're trying, Mr. Kirkland."

"I am trying," said Arthur, "and we're gonna be successful. You have my word on it."

"This is getting a little crazy, isn't it?" said McCullaugh. Hysteria was not far from the surface.

"I know," said Arthur.

"We finally got the evidence that proves I'm innocent, didn't we?"

"Yes, we did."

"I mean, it does prove it, doesn't it?"

"Conclusively. You are innocent."

"And that Judge Fleming, he agrees, right?"

Arthur nodded. He knew what was coming and knew he would have to steel himself against loss of control. The client needed maturity and confidence, someone self-assured whom he could lean on—not a lawyer as crazed and exasperated at the legal system as he was. "That's right," he said.

"Well, if everybody agrees I'm innocent," said McCullaugh, "why am I going back to jail?"

"Jeff," said Arthur carefully, "we have enough evidence to prove you're innocent, but the court will not accept that proof."

"Why not?"

"A legal technicality."

"But I'm innocent!"

"There's a law," said Arthur, "that requires evidence to be submitted within a certain time period. We got that evidence three days late."

A muscle quivered near McCullaugh's temple. "What difference does that make?"

"It's a technicality."

"What if they got the evidence three *years* late?" His voice rose. "They got the proof they need. They should let me go."

"You're right," said Arthur.

"I don't understand," said McCullaugh. He began to shiver. "I don't understand. That judge knows I'm innocent, and he's sending me back to jail." His mouth worked. "What's going on here?"

Arthur held out his hands. "Listen, you're going to get out. It's just going to take a little longer, that's all. Most judges would have overlooked the time limitation, but Fleming"—he shook his head—"that bastard goes by the letter of the law."

"But three days? *Three?*"

"To him it might just as well be three years."

McCullaugh shook his head. "It's crazy," he mumbled, "crazy. . . ."

The guard signaled for the prisoners to board the van, and the other men began to move. Arthur reached out toward McCullaugh, patted his hands, felt the icy steel handcuffs. "Just don't lose hope," said Arthur forcefully. "I'm here, and I'm working. I'll get you out."

McCullaugh looked at him silently, then moved toward the van. Arthur watched the doors close behind him.

The water on his face wasn't working. Arthur stared at himself in the mirror of the office bathroom. He needed more than water splashed from a sink to remove the lines of fatigue that were etched under his eyes. More even than sleep, though that would help. But the tiredness was the draining of years, not days, and its cause was the quality of his life and work, as well as the quantity. It was, in fact, indelible, would remain so forever. Sherry, his secretary, stood in the doorway, steno pad in hand.

". . . and Mrs. Tate wants to talk to you. Her son broke his leg again. Neighbor's driveway."

Arthur put a towel around his neck, and snatched an aerosol can from a glass shelf.

"Bricker wants to know if your client will settle for sixty thousand," continued Sherry.

Arthur tipped the can over his open palm and pressed the nozzle. Clear fluid ran over his fingers.

"You can reach him at his club," said Sherry.

Arthur shook the can vigorously and again pushed on the top.

"You've got three new clients coming in this afternoon."

A second spray of clear liquid drenched Arthur's palm.

"One whiplash," said Sherry, "one divorce, and the other one has something to do with amnesia, I forget exactly what it is."

Arthur stared dumbly at the can. Something was not right.

Sherry looked up from her pad. "Arthur, what are you doing?"

"Foam," said Arthur, dazed. "This isn't foamy."

Sherry nodded slowly. "That's because it's deodorant," she said.

Arthur studied the can. "Well," he said finally, "now that my hands don't stink I can get on with the business of shaving." He replaced the deodorant on the shelf and took out a container of shaving cream.

"I think you're getting senile," said Sherry.

"Coffee, please," said Arthur, shaking the can, then squeezing a blob of lather into his palm.

Sherry returned her gaze to the pad. She was a

buxom girl with tangerine-colored hair, a pleasant disposition, and a suggestion of buck teeth that gave her a faintly rodentlike appearance. Nevertheless, after his divorce, Arthur had considered asking her out, but was dissuaded by the example of Ernie Moskowitz, a lawyer who had recently gone into bankruptcy. The reason was that Moskowitz, married, had hired a succession of beautiful secretaries whom he spent all day making love to—instead of doing any work. "It's an object lesson," Jay had told Arthur. "Never get your meat where you get your bread." And so Arthur had decided against dating Sherry, despite the fact that he usually bought both meat and bread in the same neighborhood store.

"The Prison Expansion Committee is meeting at two o'clock," said Sherry, "Pier fourteen."

"Coffee," said Arthur, spreading the lather on his face.

"And today is Tuesday, so don't forget to visit your grandfather."

"Coffee."

"And there's a Mrs. Patterson waiting."

Arthur smiled, a pantomime face beneath shaving-cream makeup. "Coffee, please, or I'll kill you."

Mrs. Patterson, an extremely obese black woman, wore a purple-and-white floral print dress, brown men's shoes with laces, and a thin silver chain that was lost in the labyrinthine folds of her neck. Her jellied hips spilled out the open sides of the guest chair in Arthur's office, and her dark, porcine eyes darted about nervously as she spoke.

"I just got to get my divorce papers, Mr. Kirkland. I got to."

Arthur sat behind his desk and jotted notes on a lined pad. "Now, these are divorce papers, not separation papers, we're talking about, right?"

Mrs. Patterson stared at the ceiling. "I haven't got them yet, so you got to get them. I want to get remarried this weekend."

"When were you divorced, Mrs. Patterson? Do you remember the date?"

"Five years," said the black woman. "Still ain't got my papers. Five years I been waiting."

Arthur sat back. He and Jay had acquired a good reputation in Baltimore's black community as lawyers who would provide honest service at reasonable prices. Not surprisingly, many black lawyers actually resented them for it, feeling that they were somehow appropriating clients they had no right to. "You certainly should have received the papers by now," said Arthur dryly.

"Don't I know it," moaned Mrs. Patterson.

"Okay, who handled the divorce?"

Mrs. Patterson shook her head. "Don't know."

"You can't remember his name?"

"All I know is that he lived two blocks from me."

"What address?"

"Address? That was five years ago. I don't even know where *I* was living then."

Arthur stared in disbelief. Even after all his time as a lawyer, peoples casualness about affairs of vital importance to them still astounded him. "What *do* you remember?"

"Let's see," said Mrs. Patterson. Her face wrinkled, as if visually illustrating concentration. She flung an arm as big as a thigh over the back of the chair. "My husband comes home and says, 'You want a divorce? Come on, we go get it.' "

"And who did you see?" tried Arthur again.

"He lived on the third floor, and he sat in this empty room."

"But who was he?"

"He says, 'You want a divorce?' And I say, 'Damn right!' "

"Was he a lawyer?"

Mrs. Patterson's eyes glazed as she visualized the scene. "Then, he takes my husband's hand and puts it in mine . . . folded." She demonstrated the technique, using her right hand to simulate her husband's palm. "Then he pulls our hands apart and shouts, *'You are divorced!* You are *divorced!'* "

Arthur watched and listened. After a while he asked, "And what did all this cost?"

"Gave my husband twenty-five dollars to pay that man," said Mrs. Patterson softly. She shook her head. "I tell you something, Mr. Kirkland, gittin' divorced ain't as easy as I thought."

"I know what you mean," said Arthur. He felt, for no particular reason, as if he might suddenly and irrationally burst into tears.

"You divorced?" asked Mrs. Patterson, with marvelously shrewd intuition.

"Yeah."

She considered a moment. "You got your papers?"

Arthur smiled hesitantly. "Yeah."

A finger of water reaches up into Baltimore's center the way a doctor's explores the interior of a patient. It is called the Inner Harbor, and it pushes past rotting piers, crumbling warehouses, antiquated markets, and a variety of sleazy, constantly changing, port-oriented businesses. It is an area that festers with crime and decay, and even the presence, at one of the berths, of the *Constellation,* the old wooden frigate that was the first ship in the United States Navy, cannot restore the district's dignity. Recognizing this, the city fathers have decided on a thirty-year Inner Harbor redevelopment plan that involves the razing of nearly all existing structures and the establishment of parks, marinas, modern office buildings, a new home for the Maryland Academy of Sciences, and high-rise apartment houses. The cost of all this, originally projected at less than three hundred million dollars, is now expected to exceed the gross national product—provided, of course, there still is a gross national product thirty years from now.

Daniel Croft, one of the architects of the redevelop-

THE
BOOK
TRADER

BOOKS · RECORDS

501 South St.
Phila.. Pa. 19147
925·0219

ment plan, walked carefully along the immaculate deck of the ship. Alongside him was the ship's captain, dressed in formal whites, and behind him walked a group of twenty-five men and women, including Arthur and Judge Rayford. The ship was docked two piers down from the *Constellation;* the Maryland Historical Society building was clearly visible in the distance. As he approached a bulkhead, Croft turned to address the group. An elderly, severe-looking man, his voice did not carry well in the open.

"Let's face it," he said, "turning a cruise ship into a prison is a pretty unusual idea, I'll grant you that."

"It's a lunatic idea," whispered Arthur, standing with Rayford near the middle of the group.

"But we're faced with some harsh realities," continued Croft.

Arthur wondered if there were ever unharsh realities, cheerful ones that didn't require the attention of people like Croft.

"Where our prisons once allotted one hundred square feet per man, it's now down to thirty," said Croft. Next to him, the captain clenched his teeth. "In three years our projections indicate that figure will be twenty square feet, in five—who knows? If the number of criminals keeps increasing at the present rate, there will shortly be more people inside our jails than out." He paused dramatically. "Drastic problems require innovative solutions."

The captain opened a nearby door and Croft motioned the group forward. "Ladies and gentlemen, have a look at a typical cell."

A few people stepped forward and stuck their heads inside the cabin. It seemed very much like the cabin on any cruise ship, two single beds, tiny bathroom, an end table, and chair. "Makes my apartment look like shit," joked Arthur as he craned his neck.

"Of course," said Croft, "certain modifications will have to be made to maintain minimum security." He exited the cabin and watched as the group members took turns peering inside. "We'd be able to accommodate two hundred prisoners on B deck alone," he said.

"Why not extend the concept?" said Arthur to Rayford as the group walked up a flight of stairs. "Why not have prison planes, keep them aloft at all times, something like a Strategic Air Command. Or dirigibles. Prisons in the sky. Confine people in the Goodyear blimp. You could moor it anywhere. Amtrak could operate prison trains; there could be submarine jails for prisoners who tried to escape a lot. There could—"

"Control yourself, Arthur," said Rayford.

They entered a large empty room with ornate chandeliers.

"We can feed eight hundred prisoners with the present facilities here," said Croft. He motioned toward a pair of double doors. "Those lead to kitchen facilities. In the far corner there's a passageway to the bar."

"So the inmates can order martinis before their filet mignon dinners," whispered Arthur.

"... the upper deck," Croft was saying. He paused. "Well, that pretty much concludes the tour. Are there any questions?"

A woman in the group raised her hand.

"Mrs. Scott," called Croft.

"Yes. As a representative of the Inner Harbor Development Committee, I would like to know where you intend to place this prison facility."

"Well, it's already placed," answered Croft.

"You mean," said Mrs. Scott incredulously, "it's going to *stay* here?"

"Yes. That is the intention."

The woman became red-faced. "But . . . but we've spent millions and millions of dollars to rejuvenate this area. Condominiums, office buildings, restaurants, discotheques for our young . . . And now you're telling me that in the midst of all this you are planning to float eight hundred criminals?"

"More like seven hundred," said Croft imperturbed. "We don't plan to operate at capacity right away."

"But that's disastrous," said Mrs. Scott.

"Well if you don't do something," said Croft, "those seven hundred criminals are going to be out on the streets. And while you're eating in your restaurants and dancing in your discotheques, they'll be robbing your condominiums."

Judge Rayford nudged Arthur. "I gather," he whispered, "you don't approve of all this."

"I think it's wonderful," said Arthur. "I can't wait to hear you sentence someone to three years on the S.S. *Veronica*."

A woman near the back called out, "How much is all this going to cost?"

Croft looked smug. "The prison ship concept can be a reality at half the cost and a quarter of the time it would take to build a comparable facility. It provides, in fact, the largest ratio of space-volume-cost per incarcerated-man-year of any confinement facility yet built."

"A ratio to remember," said Arthur.

"What about seasickness?" asked a man.

The group laughed, but Croft remained serious. "We'll be doling out Dramamine with our prison grays. But there's really no problem. The ship is secured well enough into the harbor."

"We're not going to be voting on this in the near future, are we?" asked Mrs. Scott.

"As a matter of fact," said Croft, "it's going before the board this weekend."

"Can't we delay the decision for a while?" said Mrs. Scott. "I mean, it's not only a major step, it's a *strange* one, don't you think?"

"I think it's logical," said Croft. "A natural progression. Look . . . everyone . . . all you need remember is this: our prisons are filled to overflowing. Vicious criminals are being put back on the streets because there's no place that has the room to hold them. It's really very simple—either accept this cost-effective solution or live with the alternative."

"I say," Arthur whispered to Rayford, "we leave the streets to the criminals and put everyone else aboard cruise ships. Reward those who deserve it."

The group fell silent.

"Please continue to look around," said Croft, "and think about making some hard decisions." He paused. "I thank you all for your time."

Afterward, in the parking lot near the pier, Judge Rayford stopped in front of his Continental. "Are we getting together this weekend?" he asked Arthur, who had accompanied him.

"I don't know," said Arthur. "You're the only person I date these days."

"Come on, Arthur," said Rayford, "you promised you'd come flying with me."

Rayford, a former Marine pilot, had been badgering Arthur for months to go flying. Arthur, who hated planes, had consistently put him off, making no secret of his fears. "I gotta tell you," said Arthur now, leaning against the Lincoln, "I got this thing about height. I'm not too fond of anything that takes place off the ground."

"Oh look, for God's sake, Arthur, will you stop worrying so much. Come on, it'll be good for you. Take the kinks out of your head." He pressed his lips together. "Besides, it gets lonely. . . ."

"Take your wife," said Arthur.

Rayford got into the Continental and closed the door. "Naw," he said. "Last thing we did together was get married." He looked out at Arthur through the rolled-down window. "Come on. You promised."

Arthur couldn't remember promising, but nevertheless felt trapped. "All right," he said glumly. "What time?"

"Ten o'clock," said Rayford.

"I'll work on my will tonight."

Rayford reached into his coat and pulled his gun out of a shoulder holster. Carefully, he leaned over and opened the glove compartment.

"You always carry that thing?" asked Arthur.

Rayford bounced the revolver in his palm. "There's law and there's order," he said. "This is order."

Arthur lingered a moment, then started back toward his own car.

4

IN the evening, Arthur went to see his grandfather. He pulled slowly into the driveway of the Lewis Retirement Home and entered the nearly empty parking lot. Most of the attendants would be gone for the day by this time; a night nurse and a few orderlies would be the only ones left on duty. Arthur headed for the entrance of the two-story brick building. He hunched inside his light jacket as the late-autumn chill suffused his body. In the home, he walked quickly past the waiting room and empty reception desk and headed down a corridor toward the elevators. Doors to the staircases were kept locked to prevent the old people from falling and hurting themselves. Arthur pressed a button and the elevator door opened. It took nearly a minute before it closed. Everything in the home was specially adjusted for age and slowness. It was a world created for the feeble, the infirm, and the senile.

Arthur's grandfather was waiting on the second floor.

"Grandpa!" called Arthur.

Sam Kirkland squinted, then moved toward the elevator doors. He opened his arms wide and embraced Arthur happily. "I wasn't sure you were coming," he said. "I wasn't sure."

The old man's beard felt rough against Arthur's cheek. Razor blades weren't permitted in the home, and his grandfather's ancient electric gave a lousy shave. "How are you?" Arthur asked.

His grandfather was wearing a shirt and loose trousers. Many of the people in the home walked around all day in pajamas and robes, but not Sam Kirkland. "This isn't a hospital," he often said. "If you don't dress, you may as well lie down and die." He was one of the few residents permitted outside by himself; often he would walk for hours around the home's small grounds. He took Arthur's arm and they headed down the corridor. "I'm good," he said. "I'm fine."

"You thought I wouldn't come?"

"No, no, I knew. I knew you'd come. It's just . . . I didn't realize it was another week already. Another week."

"It's hard to keep track," said Arthur.

"Times goes fast when you're busy," said Sam. He looked up at Arthur and grinned. Both of them knew there was virtually nothing to do at the home, that it was particularly bad when the weather became colder. Sam could no longer concentrate on reading for long periods, and so many of the other residents suffered from hearing or physical problems that even finding someone to converse with was difficult.

"So," said Arthur, "everything is all right?" Occasionally Sam had complaints, and Arthur would intervene on his behalf. The television in the recreation room was not working properly. Someone had stolen the checker set. They were serving tomato soup four days a week. Arthur would speak to the director.

Sometimes the problems were corrected, sometimes not. Sometimes they went away by themselves.

Sam motioned at an old woman standing in a doorway. There were thirty-two rooms on the second floor, two residents in each. "See this one?" he said.

"Yeah," said Arthur, embarrassed. He had slowed his walk considerably so as not to outpace his grandfather's shuffle.

"A wonderful woman," said Sam. "I went to her husband's funeral. A fine man."

Arthur had never heard his grandfather speak ill of anyone; everybody was "wonderful" or "fine."

"Gitel," called Sam to the woman, "you know my grandson, Arthur?" His voice rose with pride. "He's in law school."

"I'm a lawyer," corrected Arthur.

"Don't be in such a hurry," said the woman.

Sam put his arm around Arthur's shoulders. "My grandson," he said, beaming. "This is my grandson."

They continued down the corridor.

"So," said Sam, "you remember your grandmother?"

"Yes."

"She was a marvelous woman, my wife. You remember?"

"I remember, Grandpa." His grandfather had never been the same after his wife's death. His retirement had left him depressed and bored; the death had accelerated his decline. When he had suffered a mild stroke, Arthur's parents had placed Sam in the home. "So," said Arthur, trying to change the subject, "things are pretty good, huh?"

"Yeah, pretty good." Sam rarely complained.

"You're not giving anyone a hard time, are you?"

Sam smiled slyly. "A couple times I pinch a cheek. No harm in that, right?"

"Absolutely not."

They turned a corner.

"So it's been a week," said Sam.

"Don't you remember? We went for a ride last time."

Sam nodded. "That's a good machine. Yeh. Nice. But you gotta remember always to give signals when you turn. You'll remember?"

"Yeah. Don't worry."

"Right is like this." Sam signaled for a right turn. "And left is like this." He stuck his palm straight out.

They passed the recreation room. On the sofas and chairs elderly people sat immobile, watching the color TV.

"All day long they sit," said Sam. "Some of them never get up. I think they take them down to the hearses in that position. And the fighting. Everyone wants a different program. You know what the old women want? Wrestling. You believe it? I'm telling you, you have ten different people, they want ten different channels. The funny thing is, though, when the attendant shuts the TV off for the night, nobody even moves. It's like they're hypnotized, or they don't know the difference between on and off."

"Do you watch?"

"Do I watch? Do *you* breathe? Of course I watch. What else is there to do. I'm already the checker champion."

They entered the deserted cafeteria. Sam reached into his pocket, removed a quarter, and inserted it in a vending machine that stood against one wall. A container of milk tumbled into the bottom compartment and Sam took it, plus three straws, and sat down at a table. Arthur sat opposite him.

"So," said Sam, "are you a good lawyer?"

Arthur shrugged.

"Are you honest?"

"I try," said Arthur. "I try. Sometimes I can't tell. Sometimes being honest doesn't have much to do with being a good lawyer."

Sam sipped the milk. "If you're not honest, you have nothing . . . no self-respect." He smiled and

38

swayed back and forth. A wisp of thin white hair fell across his eyebrows. "Your parents should see you now."

"To hell with them," said Arthur.

"Don't say that."

"Why?"

"It's not nice. They're still your parents."

"Yes, but that doesn't grant them eternal immunity from being judged like anyone else."

"And who's passing the judgment? You?"

Arthur nodded. "Yes," he said softly. "Judgment, but not sentence. They never cared. They wouldn't care now."

A white residue of milk appeared on Sam's lips. "Have you heard from them?"

"Of course not. Have you?"

Sam shook his head. "Take a sip of milk. You want? Take. I brought you a straw."

"I don't care about me," said Arthur. "But have they been back to see you *once* in all these years?"

Sam guffawed, as if the notion were too preposterous to even consider. "They've been busy . . . sunbathing . . . and . . . what have you."

"Everyone is busy."

"They have lives to lead. They're still young people yet."

"We all have lives," said Arthur.

"Have some milk. You look a little pale." He proffered a straw to Arthur, who took it idly.

"How can you defend them?" said Arthur. "You helped support them all those years. You think I don't know? I know. My father failed more times in business than a cat has lives, and yet we were always comfortable. I knew where the money was coming from."

"You help your children. . . ." said Sam.

Arthur peeled the end of the wrapper off the straw. He blew sharply into the opening, and the wrapper flew off and landed on another table. "We used to do

39

that in the high school lunch room," he said. "We'd dip
the ends in mashed potatoes so when we blew the
wrappers up to the ceiling, they'd stick. The place was
covered with stalactites when we left."

Sam was still eying him reproachfully.

"And after you retired, they talked you into putting
all your money in their names."

"They didn't talk me into it, I agreed. What did I
need it for? Better I should put it where someone
can use it."

"Use it to move to Arizona and stick you in an old-
age home?"

Sam's gaze fell. "At least some happiness came
from it."

"Are you happy?"

"I get along." He put the container to his lips.

"I'm sorry, Sam, I can't see it."

"All right, so don't. But you can't deny they're
your parents."

"In name only. When did I ever see them. I was
with you more than with them." Arthur slowly shook
his head. "I'm sorry, Grandpa, you're a wonderful
man, but your son is a shit."

"He was born with colic," said Sam.

Arthur laughed and reached out to touch his grandfather's cheek. "Sam . . . I love you."

Sam stared at him through watery eyes. "Look at
you. Filled out, like a man. I remember when you'd
go outside, all dressed up in your new suit, and you'd
stuff the pockets with dirt."

"I did that?"

"Sure, you did it. That was the least you did. You
were—I dunno, three, four, who remembers?—you
once stuck a knife in an electric socket, nearly killed
yourself. The whole building was blacked out for an
hour."

"I must have been a terror," said Arthur.

"You were a child, a normal boy growing up. Soon
you'll look like a lawyer and you'll be a lawyer."

"Sam," said Arthur patiently, "I am a lawyer. I've been a lawyer for twelve years."

Sam drained the milk, put down the container. "Twelve years is nothing."

"To me it's a lot."

"I had my specialty shop for *fifty* years. Can you imagine, Arthur, *fifty years.*"

"It's incredible."

"You could get anything: a watch, pair of shoes, a zipper—what didn't I carry? You remember?"

"Sure I do." And Arthur did. From age five to fifteen he had spent half his life in that store. First, as a child, left there so his parents could have some freedom, fascinated by the infinite variety of the merchandise; next as a young helper and occasional (to his later great shame) thief; and, finally, as a paid salesman and assistant. Then he discovered girls.

"Zippers and aspirins," said Sam, "it's been a good life. I can't complain." He chuckled. "But not like being a lawyer, eh?" He gripped Arthur's wrists with wrinkled, mottled hands.

"What could compare to that?" said Arthur.

Sam sat back and thought a moment in silence. An orderly began turning off the overhead fluorescents. "So," said Sam, "it's been a week already."

One by one, the lights winked out.

It was dark when Arthur returned to his apartment. The security guard greeted him from his desk in the lobby.

"Evening, Mr. Kirkland."

Arthur nodded. "How you doing, Edwin?"

"Oh, not bad. You in for the rest of the night?" He glanced up at a clock on the wall. The time was nine-twenty.

"Yeah," said Arthur. He headed for the bank of elevators.

"If anyone comes in," called the guard, "you want me to send them on up?"

"Shoot them," Arthur called back. "No one is coming."

"Night, Mr. Kirkland."

"Night."

Arthur stood in the shower and let the warm water splash on his face. He had just completed his second soaping with dandruff shampoo, and his head felt like a prune. For the first time in his life he had noticed dandruff on his suit jackets and had decided to take counter-maneuvers. His hair was getting progressively more oily, difficult to comb. A sign of age, Jay had told him. Metabolism changing. Body marking the passage to midlife. Soon there would be a weight gain of five to ten pounds, a little bursitis in the left shoulder, maybe some lower-back pain—and before he knew it, the Big Trip.

Arthur stopped the shower, got out of the tub, toweled himself dry. Not yet, he thought. Not just yet. In the bedroom, still nude, he used a hot-comb to style his hair. He had four hot-combs, three of which were broken and which he was always reminding himself to have fixed. He put on a pair of black socks and boxer shorts and shuffled into the living room. He felt the shag of the thick baby-blue carpet poking up between his toes as he walked to the room's lone piece of furniture, and sat down. The leather easy chair and the large potted plant behind it were the only souvenirs of his marriage. In the seven years since he had last seen Helene, he had somehow never gotten around to redecorating.

This had been one of Helene's complaints—his lack of interest in the apartment. Helene had entire lists of complaints, constantly updated, an ongoing assessment of their marriage. Arthur had to admit most of the charges were valid. He frequently did not make it home for dinner, often failed to call. He was irritable and moody—he brought to his personal life the torments of the office. He was uncultured; he rarely read a book, preferred a Colts game to a concert or play. They both realized after several years that their marriage was doomed. The charm, mutual intelligence, and physical attractiveness that had brought them together were insufficient to bind them permanently. They could not have children for reasons that baffled even eminent specialists. For his part, Arthur had simply grown tired of it all, weary of the strain of trying to please her, wanting only to be left alone.

"You're a hermit!" she accused. "So go be a hermit, see how you like it!"

He liked it. Basically he was a loner. He dipped into the social world now whenever *he* felt like it, when he needed sex or when he was lonely or when he wanted excitement. More often, he was alone, content and comfortable with himself. He was good company. He had given Helene everything, including generous alimony. The divorce was "amicable"— meaning the despondency, rage, and heartache were kept muffled below the surface. At their final meeting, in her lawyer's office, Arthur had gently kissed Helene good-bye. All that remained was the leather chair.

Arthur leaned back until the leaves of the potted plant brushed the top of his head. Sometimes he pretended they were the fingers of a woman in the process of giving him a massage. "A little lower," he whispered, "and more to the right." The plant had dark-green foliage and thick, woody branches. Arthur wondered what type it was; Helene had told him a hundred times but he could never remember. That was another one of her complaints, and because of it, she'd grown to hate the plant. Abruptly, Arthur stood up. He was hungry. He walked to the kitchen, took a box of Mallomars from the refrigerator, and opened it. Six cookies were left. He ate them all. He saw some dishes in the sink, decided to leave them there. He would wash them in the morning. His dishwasher had been broken for three months. One of these days, he thought, I really have to get that thing fixed.

He returned to the bedroom. A group of Manila folders and loose papers were scattered near the foot of the bed. The Elliot files . . . the manufacturer of shoe horns, who was suing his mother for opening a competing business. Arthur made note to return the files in the morning. He climbed into the bed, removed a pair of glasses from the night table, and put them on. Crawling to the edge of the mattress, he reached out to the television three feet away and flipped the switch. There were sounds of shooting and sirens, and a wavery, indecipherable picture. The TV had been defective for a long time—a bad tuner, a technician-neighbor had told him—and often, Arthur watched for hours with his hand against the channel selector, having found that a steady pressure, if applied just right, could produce an acceptable picture. But now he felt tired, unable and unwilling to hold onto the tuner. The screen flickered awhile and then went black. "Shit," said Arthur resignedly.

He removed his glasses and sat absolutely still. The shooting and sirens continued.

Perspiration ran out from under Ovitz's toupee, trickled down his forehead, entered the forests of his sideburns, and emerged in the fleshy clearings of his neck. Ovitz's fingers drummed relentlessly on the table in front of him and his voice stuck in his throat as he attempted to speak into the microphone. Twenty feet away, William Zinoff, chairman of the Ethics Committee waited impatiently. He sat with his five associates at an immense wood table in the impressively large hearings room at City Hall, a room whose ornate chandeliers, tiled floors, and velvet-curtained windows made it seem more appropriate for a wedding reception than for the current proceedings. Zinoff looked up from a yellow pad.

"Shall I repeat the question, Mr. Ovitz?" he asked.

The mike in front of him sent his voice booming through the hall.

"Yes," said Ovitz nervously. "I heard it, but maybe a repetition would drive it home."

"Very well," said Zinoff, who could use phrases like that without seeming self-conscious. "Do you know Walter Kimball?"

"You mean know personally?"

Zinoff's snow-white hair seemed to stiffen on his leonine head. He conceded nothing. "I mean, do you know him?"

Ovitz coughed up some phlegm into a tissue. "Yes. I do know him."

Next to Zinoff, Barney Cecil adjusted his microphone. Like most of the other committee members, he could only get it to be either too loud or too soft. He selected too soft. "He was a member of your real estate group, isn't that correct?"

Ovitz placed a hand to his ear, pantomimed not hearing.

Cecil adjusted his mike for too loud and repeated the question.

"It was not *my* real estate group," said Ovitz. "I was simply an investor, as were the others."

"As was Walter Kimball?"

"Yes, as far as I knew."

"And this group," said Harvey Crenna, puffing a pipe near the end of the table, "this group was formed for the purpose of speculating in commercial real-estate ventures that included the purchase of a number of properties, is that right?"

"I would use the term 'investing' rather than speculating," said Ovitz. "But the rest is substantially correct."

"And is it also correct," said Cecil, "that one of these properties—"

Ovitz again held his ear.

Gail Packer, the lone woman on the committee, leaned over to adjust Cecil's mike. There was a hum, then silence. Cecil looked up from her cleavage. "It is also correct that one of these properties was used as a massage parlor, is it not?"

Ovitz inhaled deeply; his sigh filled the hall. "Yes, that is correct."

"And that acts of prostitution did take place in that establishment?"

"So I've been given to understand," said Ovitz wearily. He wiped his forehead with a handkerchief. "But I must state again to this committee that I was just an investor in a general commercial venture and had no personal knowledge of this particular activity."

"You didn't know what was going on on your own property?" asked Crenna.

"No, sir," said Ovitz. "Of course not. Had I known of this, I not only would have terminated my involvement but I would have reported it to the authorities."

"And jeopardized your rental income and profits?"

"Yes," shouted Ovitz. His microphone squealed deafeningly. "Sorry," he said quietly. "Yes." He shook his head. "My career as a lawyer is too important to risk it for a few dollars. The whole thing— it's ridiculous." He paused, searching, hands clutching the air in front of him. "I don't know what else to tell you."

Zinoff looked at him coldly. "It is your contention, then, that you were unaware of illegal activities— prostitution—taking place on premises that you co-owned."

"Yes, sir."

Zinoff put his hand over the mike and leaned backward. The other members of the committee did the same, as Zinoff spoke to them. Ovitz looked around the vast empty hall, silent now except for a low electronic hum. He saw the people at the large table nod their heads, all except Gail Packer. Zinoff removed his hand from the microphone.

"Mr. Ovitz, it is the opinion of this committee that you were, in fact, part of a conspiracy to allow the illegal operations on your property to occur. Such naïveté as you profess—particularly on the part of a member of the legal profession—simply does not carry the weight of credibility. We feel there is more than enough evidence to prove this conclusion."

"But I didn't know!" wailed Ovitz. His head seemed to shake uncontrollably.

"I am sorry, Mr. Ovitz," Zinoff continued sternly, "but the committee is going to advocate disbarment proceedings."

"Disbarment . . ." echoed Ovitz unbelievingly.

"If you wish to avoid the embarrassment of such proceedings, you may request voluntary disbarment." He stood up. "We'll take a short recess," said Zinoff flatly.

The committee members quickly rose and filed toward a rear exit. Ovitz slowly gathered up several papers in front of him and placed them in an attaché case next to his chair. Then, dazed, he stood up and shuffled toward the entrance by which he had come in. His eyes were unfocused as he pushed open the large ornamented doors.

Arthur was waiting in the hall. "So, how'd it go?"

Ovitz stared at him lifelessly. "They just slit my throat. It's all over. I'm finished."

"What do you mean?"

"I'm going to have to ask for voluntary disbarment," said Ovitz.

Arthur shook his head in disbelief. "Vol— For what? Holy sh— What'd you do?"

Ovitz shrugged. "I did nothing. Arthur, I didn't do anything, I swear."

"But that's crazy. . . ."

"What do I do now?" said Ovitz. "Tell me. You've been around. What do I do? I have a wife and kids, and I've been a lawyer for eighteen years. What do I do? Lay bricks?"

Arthur looked at the ceiling, and remained silent. His own questioning proceeded for forty minutes, the first ten centering on his contempt citations, the last thirty covering a rambling range of acquaintances, rumors, and innuendoes. Arthur sat at the same small table that Ovitz had.

"Do you know Jules Stouffer?" asked Cecil.

"Yes, I do," said Arthur.

Cecil squinted at some notes in front of him. "He was a client of yours, isn't that right?"

"That is correct," said Arthur.

"Wasn't he originally represented by Alvin Burton? That is, before he came to you?"

"Yes."

"Why did he change representation?"

"He didn't," said Arthur.

"You just said he came to you after Mr. Burton," interjected Gail Packer. Arthur had noticed her staring at him during the questioning, not only at his face but his hands and chest. Once he had caught her eye and held his own gaze until she looked away.

"It wasn't a change in representation," said Arthur. "It was an addition to his representation. He came to me with an accident case. I'm more familiar with that area than Burton."

"Did Jules Stouffer express dissatisfaction with Mr. Burton?" said Cecil.

"No."

"He didn't at any time tell you that he was unhappy with Burton's representation?" Cecil pressed.

"No. He never did," replied Arthur.

"Then your testimony," continued Cecil, "is that Stouffer never told you he was unhappy with Burton."

"Never," said Arthur, his voice rising. "Look, Burton's an excellent lawyer. You're not going after him, are you?"

Zinoff, eyes flashing, reached out to pull a microphone from across the table. The amplified rasp sent shudders through everyone in the hall. "We are not 'going after' anyone, Mr. Kirkland. We are simply—"

"Do you know David Crebbs?" interrupted a ferret-

48

faced man who hadn't previously spoken. His name was Aaron Polic, and he wore a bow tie.

Zinoff glanced at him angrily. "We are simply trying to review certain accusations," he continued, "to determine whether or not they are true."

"In other words, you are trying these people in absentia," said Arthur. "Is that what it is?"

"Everyone accused of anything is entitled to appear before this committee," countered Zinoff.

"But not to confront their accusers, or to cross-examine them, or—"

"Mr. Kirkland, we are not a court of law here. We are merely attempting—under very difficult conditions, I might add—to more or less clean our own house before someone comes in and does it for us. All professional organizations have similar problems and practices, so please do not overdramatize these proceedings. We have enough histrionics as it is. These are not the McCarthy hearings."

Arthur raised his eyebrows theatrically. "Oh, that's a relief. So the next question is not going to be 'Are you now or have you ever been a lawyer?'"

"That is not amusing, Mr. Kirkland," said Gail Packer.

"Do you know David Crebbs?" repeated Polic.

Arthur ignored him. He was studying Gail Packer's cheekbones and wondering what she was doing here on this panel of stodgy old men. "You're absolutely right, Miss, uh . . ."

"Packer," said Gail.

"Miss Packer," echoed Arthur. He noticed she had gray-green eyes and chiseled features. He let his gaze drop to her full bustline, his imagination working on what was below the table. You could never tell. Disappointment lurked everywhere. How many women were gazelles from the waist up, hippos from the waist down? Slim shoulders, but thighs like bridge abutments? Sometimes it was better not to know. . . . "None of this is amusing," he said, "but it *is* ridiculous. Ludicrous, I think, considering the profession of those engaged in it." He turned back to Polic, who was smoothing his bow tie. "In answer to your question, sir, yes. Yes, I do know David Crebbs."

"Have you ever seen him—" Polic tapped the microphone. "Is this [inaudible] thing working?" He moved closer to it, his ferret snout nearly touching the metal. "Do you know David Crebbs?" A sudden whine of the microphone approached the pain level of human hearing.

Arthur covered his ears. "I can hear you."

Polic backed off.

"Why are we using the microphones?" said Arthur. "There are only six of us here. Why don't we just move our tables a little closer."

Beefy, red-faced committeeman Daniel Gallagher explained. "This is a hearing," he said.

"Ah," said Arthur. "I see. A hearing."

Harvey Crenna uncovered a torn yellow sheet from under the piles of paper in front of him. He read it carefully. "Do you know Jules Stouffer?" he said, looking sharply at Arthur.

Arthur grinned.

Zinoff shielded his microphone and leaned backward. "We've already covered that, Mr. Crenna."

Crenna knitted his brows. "We covered Stouffer?"

"Yes."

"Well then, how about Alvin Burton?"

Zinoff nodded.

Crenna again leaned over his mike. "Mr. Kirkland," he said portentiously, "I'd like to ask you at this time if you've ever heard of a man named David Crebbs."

"I just asked that," said Polic, his nose twitching.

Crenna had a sudden insight. Polic looks like a squirrel, he thought. A squirrel in a bow tie. "What did he say?"

"He said yes," interjected Arthur.

Polic stared at him through beady eyes. "Have you ever seen him intoxicated in court?"

"He slurs his words because he has a speech impediment," said Arthur angrily. "I'm sure if you checked your records it would be in there somewhere."

"The question, Mr. Kirkland, is—"

"The answer is no," said Arthur, his voice rising. "No, I haven't seen him intoxicated. No, he does not drink, does not drink at all." He paused and took a deep breath. "At this point, I would like to say that in theory what this committee is trying to do is highly commendable. However, in practice, it sucks."

"Mr. Kirkland—"

"I will not answer any further questions," said Arthur. He nodded once, and stood up.

Outside, in the corridor, Arthur stooped over a water fountain. The stream felt cold against his teeth. It had been a year and a half since he had last been to the dentist; he made a mental note to make an appointment. He became aware that someone was speaking to him.

"What do you think we're trying to do in there?"

Arthur glanced up briefly, saw Gail Packer standing over him, then continued drinking. He did, however, observe her bottom half—slim, shapely legs, good calves and ankles. Now if only her ass were not a disappointment . . . He straightened finally and dabbed at several drops on his chin with the tip of his tie. "You want some water?" he asked.

"Whatever you may think," said Gail, "we are not witch-hunting."

"Then what are you doing?"

"There's a lot of corruption that no one's taking any steps to alleviate."

"And you think your committee is doing something about it?"

"Yes."

Arthur nodded slowly, looked at the floor, and then raised his eyes. "That committee," he said deliberately, "is a very dangerous farce."

Gail made a quick motion with her neck that sent her hair whirling past her shoulders.

I wonder if that's what they mean by "tossing one's head," thought Arthur. The phrase had somehow always conjured up images of volleyball, or women bowlers.

"You really like to attack, don't you?" she was saying. "I spend fourteen hours a day working for that committee—"

"I don't care how many hours you spend."

"—and I don't do it because I think it will give me some good laughs."

"I'm not laughing, believe me."

"You know as well as I do that if we don't police our own activities, *nothing* will change, noth—"

"Oh, things will change, all right. You'll end up ruining the careers of—"

"—nothing will get done, and—"

"—a few little guys who happened to wipe their asses the wrong way. But—"

"—the goddamn corruption will just go on!" She stared at him defiantly.

"—other than that," continued Arthur, his voice quieting, "nothing."

She was fuming.

Arthur smiled. He waited as the look of confusion spread over her small face. "So, what do you think?"

She *tossed her head*. "About what?"

"You think I'm kind of a . . . nice guy? Somebody you want to have a drink with . . . or something?"

Gail's surprise slowly changed to sly amusement. "Okay," she said slowly. "Where?"

"Daniel's? Seven-thirty?"

"Eight."

She walked away. Her ass, Arthur saw, was splendid.

ONE step behind a police guard, Arthur walked briskly down the corridor until they came to a faded-green door. The guard's keys jingled as he opened it. "Twenty minutes," he said. Arthur waved, and entered.

Inside, seated at a table, was Ralph Agee, the black transvestite Arthur had seen humiliated in the lock-up the day before. He was still wearing the pale-blue dress, but the blond wig was gone. Arthur heard the door being locked behind him. He set his briefcase on the table as Agee slowly turned. Arthur extended his hand.

"I'm Arthur Kirkland. You wanted to see me?"

Agee shook it gently. "Yeah. My man, Bambi, recommended you real highly. Says you the man to see."

Arthur sat down. The room's furnishings consisted of only a table and two chairs. It reminded Arthur of his living room. "Okay, Ralph, why don't you tell me what happened?" Arthur removed a folder and a legal pad from the briefcase.

"Cops tell you their side?"

"My report says you were involved in a robbery," said Arthur. "That true?"

"No, sir," said Agee, shaking his head emphatically. "What happened is, it was time to come down on a nigger. You know, it's like smoking. They gotta have a nigger every twenty minutes."

"I want to know what actually went on."

Agee extended a tapered index finger. "What it

was is, I was in this alley, petting my dog, when they came down on me."

Arthur flipped open the folder, found a particular page, and scanned it quickly. He looked up. "It says here the dog was *attacking* you when the policemen arrived on the scene."

"Well," said Agee, "my dog gets that way sometimes. He gets excited. . . ."

"It states here the animal belongs to a Mrs. B. Jackson."

Agee's eyes widened. "He sure looked like my dog."

Arthur tilted his head in cynical disbelief.

"Got that"—Agee pointed to his forehead in a futile effort to describe the dog's markings—"you know, that, uh . . ."

Arthur slowly shook his head. Agee was a most unsophisticated liar. "Come on, Ralph. It also states"—he read from the page in front of him—"'When asked what he was doing in the alley, the suspect stated *I don't know nothing about no taxicab robbery.*'"

"That's right," said Agee. "I don't."

"How'd you know there was one?"

"'Cause there's always one."

Arthur stood up and began gathering his papers. "Listen, Ralph, you either tell me what happened or you get yourself another lawyer, because I don't have time for this bullshit." He stuffed the papers in his briefcase and headed for the door.

"Wait a minute!"

Arthur's hand was on the knob. (Actually, the door wouldn't have opened. He had to knock for the guard.)

"All right," said Agee. "I was in that cab, but I didn't rob it."

Arthur stopped and slowly turned. He had played this charade a hundred times, maybe a thousand. New-car buyer trying to wheedle the last few bucks from the salesman. Let's make a deal. The procedure was almost codified, a Japanese play acted out by lawyers and criminals. "Who did rob it?" asked Arthur, still poised at the door.

"My cousin," said Agee quickly. "My cousin did it. I didn't know nothin'. It was my cousin's idea, an' that man is crazy."

"What's your cousin's name?"

"I don't know, but he lives up on Hillsdale."

"You don't know your cousin's name?" Act Two coming up, thought Arthur. He swiveled again and drew back his hand to knock on the door.

"Hey!" said Agee. "Where you goin' now? I'm tellin' you the truth."

Arthur stared at him angrily. "Hey, I don't need this. What do you think I am, an idiot?"

"No, I don't—"

"I read a report, I can tell if someone's bullshitting me. I don't need this crap. You either give me some straight answers or you get yourself another lawyer."

"I don't know no other lawyer."

"Well, then that's tough. I've got better things to do than listen to this jive-ass put-on." He knocked on the door, but lightly.

"Okay, okay," said Agee quickly. "No bullshit. No bullshit."

Arthur stopped the knocking, smoothed his collar, headed slowly back toward the table. Okay, he thought. Maybe now we can get at the truth. No more bluffing. He sat down, opened the briefcase, again brought out the pad and folder. "So what do you have to tell me?"

"Well, it wasn't my idea," said Agee, "but I knew what was comin' down. Me and my cousin—"

Arthur looked at him sharply.

"Royce. Royce Shavers."

Arthur wrote down the name.

"He figures that since . . . since I am the way I

am . . ." He paused. A grin flickered across his lips. "I can look real fine sometimes, you know . . . ?"

"I'm sure you can."

"He figures we can be a couple."

"A man and a woman."

"Yeah, that's it. Man and woman couple. Cab drivers will pick up a couple a whole lot faster than two nigger men."

"Where did you hail the cab?" asked Arthur.

"What?"

"Where did you first get in the cab."

"We got in over on Garrison Boulevard and we, uh . . . we . . ." The tears welled in Agee's eyes.

Arthur, taking notes, did not notice. "We what?" he asked impatiently.

"We asked him to take us down to the . . . to the harbor. You know, like . . . we was tourists, and uh . . . we . . ." His voice broke and he began to shake his head.

Arthur looked up finally and offered a handkerchief.

Agee wiped his eyes. "Man, I can't go to jail. That place . . . I can't do it. I can't, man. You gotta help me, please. You gotta help me."

Ten minutes later, Agee was led away by one of the guards. He seemed petrified, nearly catatonic. "Don't worry," said Arthur softly. "I'm on your case. You'll be out on bail within the hour."

Agee whimpered but made no response.

The main hall in the lock-up was, as usual, a noisy amalgam of criminals and lawyers, victims and detectives, bail bondsmen and reporters. People cried and complained, whispered deals and shouted protests, went willingly or resisted maniacally—it was always the same. Arthur was threading his way through the mass of humanity when he heard his name called. A bulky figure detached itself from the crowd and waddled toward him. Warren Fresnell.

"I have," said Fresnell, *"the* most fantastic news you've ever heard."

"What is it? You got a second mortgage on that house, or something?" asked Arthur.

"Guess who the police just brought in."

"Who?"

"Guess."

"Warren, I'm really not in any mood to play your games."

"Judge Fleming."

Arthur's mind jumped to attention. "What?"

"Just brought in. I know it sounds crazy."

"What do you mean, 'brought in'?"

Fresnell smiled self-importantly. "Arrested!"

Arthur, regaining his senses, shook his head. "Nice try."

"You think I'm kidding?"

"Of course."

"I'm not. I'm telling you. They arrested the judge."

Arthur felt lightheaded; a tingling began in his chest. "Judge Fleming?" he said slowly, trying to concentrate.

"Judge Fleming. Your very own favorite judge."

Arthur rejected believing what he had heard. "Okay, what's the punch line?"

"What?"

"The punch line. The joke. Is there a joke connected to this?"

Fresnell pressed his lips together. "You know, Kirkland, if you were on fire and I came over to help put out the flames, you'd first make me sign a release in triplicate. Did you ever ask yourself when natural suspicion and caution cross the border into paranoia?"

"I did," said Arthur, "but I didn't believe the answer." He paused. "All right, I'm sorry. Exactly what happened?"

"I don't know," said Fresnell. "Except that it's no joke. Nobody knows what it's about. They've got the whole thing bottled up. I can't get anything from any-body."

Arthur held up a palm as he spotted a familiar face across the hall. "Mathews!" he called out. Mathews, the booking officer, looked around, spotted Arthur and Fresnell, and waved. Arthur motioned him toward them.

"Morning, gents," Mathews said cheerfully as he ap-proached them. "Fine day out, huh?" Mathews always said this, regardless of the weather.

"This may conceivably be the finest day of the year," said Arthur. He leaned in conspiratorially. "Listen, uh, what's this with Fleming? You got him down here?"

Mathews's face reddened. He knew Arthur reason-ably well, not only from seeing him around the lock-up, both as prisoner and as attorney, but also because Arthur had once represented Mathews's brother in a tax fraud case. "I don't know anything about it," he said.

Arthur placed his hand on Mathews's shoulder. "Hey, Gil, come on. It's me you're talking to. Arthur."

"Wouldn't matter if you were Jane Fonda in a shorty nightgown," said Mathews. "Answer's the same."

Arthur tried to make his voice sound sincere. "Seri-ously, I'd like to know. Is he here?"

"You really wanna know?" said Mathews softly.

Arthur leaned in even closer. "Yes. Yes, I do."

"I don't know!" boomed Mathews. He stalked off.

Arthur turned to Fresnell. "Something's hot. If you hear anything, let me know."

Fresnell moved away. "You'll be the first," he said.

Jay Porter stood up and slowly gathered his papers. A short recess had been announced in Courtroom D before the next case. The present case was over, and Jay had won. But, as so often happened, he felt neither pride nor relief. His client, John Simms, was guilty of murder. He was running a cocaine bagging and dealing operation with his common-law wife when one day she decided to leave and go into business for herself. Three weeks later, before the eyes of her two horrified children, Simms had deliberately run the woman down with his automobile. She died in the street.

Jay had pulled out all the stops. Although a police search of Simms's apartment had turned up a few ounces of cocaine, there was no real evidence that he was a dealer. He had no past criminal record, and association with known narcotics users could not be proven. At the police station he had been put into a line-up before a lawyer was present. A jailhouse reporter had taken his picture despite his attempt to turn away, and it had appeared in the next day's paper with the caption ACCUSED WIFE-MURDERER. At the booking, again before Jay was on the case, Simms had identified the victim as his wife. Almost immediately, Jay began with the motions. He made a discovery motion demanding access to the DA's evidence. (The assistant DA on the case, Morton Tipton, was going for first-degree murder, and would not listen to any deals.) Jay made a motion to suppress the drug evidence on the grounds it was illegally acquired. He made a motion to quash the indictment based on prejudicial pretrial publicity. He made a motion to challenge the selection process of the grand jury. (Simms was young and black, the jury mostly elderly and white.) He made a motion for an indefinite continuance, asking for substantial delays. ("You've made more motions on this case than all your others combined," Arthur had told him.)

In the end, Tipton had yielded. His principal witnesses, Simms's wife's children (by a former marriage), were required to testify about both the homicide and their mother's walkout on the drug operation. By mid-trial, Jay had seriously confused them on the witness stand. He had threatened Tipton with asking for a directed verdict of acquittal, and both men knew he had a reasonable chance of getting it. Tipton had agreed to a guilty plea for voluntary manslaughter—homicide committed in the heat of passion. The murder charge, which demanded proof of premeditation, would be dropped. The judge had gone along. Sentence would be the three years Simms had already served, plus five years on parole.

Simms stood up and stretched. "Man," he said to Jay, "you sure pulled a number there."

Jay said nothing.

"I thought for sure I was gonna be doin' more time."

Jay snapped his briefcase shut. "You should be, you asshole."

Simms smoothed some hairs on his wispy mustache. "Hey, I'm real grateful."

"Yeah," said Jay. "Right."

Simms extended a hand to shake, but Jay pretended not to see. "I'm gonna go out an' hoist me a few," said Simms. "Wanna come? I could show you some good ways to relax."

Jay looked at Simms's eyes. In addition to the usual cunning and even cruelty, there seemed to be something else there, something glittering that was barely held in check, an icy sparkle of surging irrationality. "I don't think so," said Jay.

Simms shrugged, and left. The bailiff approached the defense table.

"Mr. Porter?"

Jay, still partially mesmerized, turned.

"Mr. Porter, your office wants you to get in touch immediately."

Jay nodded. "Thanks, Harry," he said vacantly.

But the image of Simms's eyes lingered in his mind.

Arthur, in Courtroom A, felt himself beginning to doze off. The room was virtually empty, except for the principals in the case and the judge. Arthur's client was

Gino Tuminaro, a man in his sixties, accused of operating premises for the purpose of prostitution. It was
true. The old man was a madam. He explained to
Arthur that he needed income to supplement his social security. The prosecutor, Allan Becker, had a
woman neighbor on the stand. He thumbed through
voluminous notes as he spoke.

". . . and . . . and you didn't notice anything, not one
thing, that would, uh, you know, uh . . . cause, mmm,
suspicion on your behalf?" He cleared his throat.

"No," said the woman.

Becker nodded his head as if pondering some pro-
fundity. His speech was so slow and hesitant that the
judge, witness, and Arthur often forgot the beginning
of his question by the time he reached the end. In
conversations with Jay, Arthur had referred to Becker
as the Human Sleeping Pill.

The judge looked up at the clock as Becker once
more consulted his notes. "Is that all, Mr. Becker?"

"What?"

"I asked, 'Is that all?' Have you completed your
questioning?"

Arthur shook himself awake.

"Uh . . . let's see," said Becker. He shook his head.
"No. No, I haven't, Your Honor."

"All right, then proceed," said the judge.

Becker nodded vigorously. "Mrs. Politnikoff," he
said forcefully. "Could—"

"Pola*t*nikoff," corrected the woman.

"Polatnikoff," said Becker. "Couldn't you . . .
couldn't you have been distracted?"

Arthur yawned.

"By what?" asked the woman.

Becker concentrated, then dipped his head back into
his notes. The bailiff cleared his throat. Mr. Tuminaro
seemed to be asleep. Becker's head finally bobbed up.
"By, mmm, the normal distractions."

Arthur moaned involuntarily. He thought now he understood why Judge Rayford always carried a gun.

As it happened, one floor below in Courtroom C, the case before Rayford was a great deal more interesting. A police officer was on the stand, and a very meek-looking, professorial forty-year-old man sat at the defense table with his lawyer, Warren Fresnell. Fresnell wore a green jacket and powder-blue trousers.

"I told him to move on," the officer was saying, "but he continued to use profanity and refused to leave the premises. My only choice was to take him into custody."

"What sort of profanity did he use?" Rayford asked. The defendant looked so dignified and clean-cut that it was barely possible to imagine him even raising his voice.

The officer hesitated. "Well, you know, uh, the normal type of . . ."

"Come on, McNally," snapped Rayford. "We're all adults here. We've all heard those words before. For the record now, what did he say?"

The officer removed a small notepad from his shirt pocket. He flipped through several pages, and then began to quietly read. "He used the word 'fuck' a lot. And 'piss on you.' " McNally looked up.

"Is that all?" asked Rayford.

McNally lowered his eyes. "He said he was going to 'bunghole' the short-order chef."

"What? Speak up, please."

"Bunghole the chef," said McNally. "He also threatened to 'cream' on the waitress . . . and stuff like that, Your Honor."

From the defense table, the defendant called out weakly, "There's a very good reason for all that, Your Honor."

Rayford regarded him bemusedly. "Oh, really. What is that?"

The defendant smoothed his tie. "I happen to be a diabetic."

Jay Porter entered the courtroom and quietly looked around. He spotted Warren Fresnell at the defense table and walked down the aisle toward him. Rayford was shaking his head.

"I fail to see the connection. I have never heard of diabetes causing foul language."

A hesitant smile appeared on the defendant's face. "May I suggest," he said, "that that is because you are a douche bag."

Rayford shook his head as Jay approached Fresnell. "Where's Arthur?" whispered Jay.

"One second," said Fresnell. "Your Honor," he intoned, facing Rayford, "Counsel requests permission to approach the bench."

"I thought he was supposed to be here," whispered Jay.

"No," Fresnell whispered back, "he's over in Courtroom A."

"Permission granted," said Rayford.

"When you're through," Jay whispered to Fresnell, "come on outside."

"I'll be through in a sec," said Fresnell. "Wait up."

"I've got something to tell you," said Jay. "You are going to flip over this."

Fresnell leaned down to his client. "I'm going to speak to the judge to see if I can get a postponement. Hang tough."

"Good luck, prick," said the defendant.

Fresnell approached the bench. "Your Honor," he said to Rayford, "I believe my client is suffering from an unusual brain illness called Gilles de la Tourette's disease. One of the symptoms is a virtually irresistible compulsion to utter profanities and obscenities. Normally, my client takes medication to alleviate these symptoms, a chemical called haloperidol, but on the evening of his arrest he had unfortunately run out of it."

Rayford looked skeptical. "I never heard of that type of illness."

"Nevertheless, Your Honor, it does exist. And my client has it."

Rayford thought a moment. "All right, Mr. Fresnell, we'll see if we can verify your contention." He signaled to the bailiff. "See that the defendant gets over to Sinai Hospital this afternoon for psychiatric observation. I will withhold the verdict pending a medical report." He rapped his gavel.

"Court is adjourned," said the bailiff.

The defendant leaned over to Fresnell as he passed. "What'd you say?"

"Told him if he didn't give us a postponement he was a fuckin' asshole," whispered Fresnell. He headed up the aisle to where Jay waited at the door.

The defendant winked.

Becker was still questioning the woman witness. She had been on the stand nearly half an hour and had not said one thing that was germane to the prosecutor's case. The judge's breathing had become slow and regular, his eyes unfocused; Arthur felt certain he was asleep. Arthur himself was becoming crazed with impatience. On the pad in front of him he had completed poorly drawn sketches of everyone in the courtroom and three-dimensional letterings of their names. He had done isometric tensing of all the major skeletal muscles in his body. He had given up trying to find the general solution of a cubic equation. He had mentally undressed, item by item of clothing, each of the women he'd gone out with in the past year. He had timed himself to see how long he could hold his breath. He felt now that he was going to snap. He remembered stories of a Greek martyr who had been imprisoned for fourteen years, forced for all that time to lie on his back in a pitch-black cave fissure no larger than a coffin. Living death, thought Arthur. A new prosecution tactic. He would finally jump to his feet screaming, "I yield, I yield the case!" and Becker would have won. Victory through enforced boredom, one for the law books.

"Did you see anything unusual?" asked Becker of the witness.

The woman sneered. "No."

"Nothing out of the ordinary?"

"I told you, no," said the woman.

Becker puckered his lips, shuffled through another ream of papers. A barely audible humming sound came from his lips.

Perhaps Becker is a machine, thought Arthur. A drone robot whose bearings needed oiling, his machine voice a forty-five record that somehow was being played at thirty-three and a third. Tuminaro, Arthur's client, leaned over to whisper in his ear.

"I be an old man before this guy gets through."

"He can't go on too much longer," said Arthur. "There'll be mass suicides soon."

"I think," said Tuminaro, "it be more easy to spend the time in prison than to sit through this trial."

"Did you hear any noise?" asked Becker brightly, as if suddenly hitting on a brilliant new line of questioning.

"No," said the woman. She looked pleadingly up at the judge, who gave no sign of seeing her.

"No noise," said Becker, nodding sagely.

At the rear of the courtroom the door opened quietly as Jay Porter and Warren Fresnell looked in. Porter was grinning widely and Fresnell was choking back laughter. Seeing Arthur in the middle of a case, they backed away into the corridor.

"No noise," repeated Becker. "You're sure now?"

"Yes."

Becker clasped his hands behind him and paced pensively in front of the witness stand. He thinks he's Clarence Darrow, F. Lee Bailey, and Percy Foreman, thought Arthur. All combined in one skinny body.

"What about," said Becker, "the uh . . . that woman . . . the blond-haired woman . . ."

"What woman?" asked the witness.

Arthur snapped. He flung his twenty-cent ball-point pen on the table and stood up. "Your Honor," he said loudly, "I would like to move that this case be dismissed for lack of evidence."

The judge's head bounced up. "Granted."

Becker knitted his brow. "Your Honor, I'm stunned. I think there is more than enough cause to—"

"Case dismissed," growled the judge. He rapped the gavel with more force than necessary, and stood up. He gave Becker a sharp look before exiting to his chambers. The assistant DA slowly shuffled back to the prosecution table and began to gather up his papers. He did not see Arthur and Tuminaro shake hands; nor did he see Arthur approach.

"I shouldn't have won this one," said Arthur angrily.

"You're telling me!" said Becker, bending to retrieve some fallen documents.

"My client is a nice guy, but I shouldn't have won," repeated Arthur. "Actually, I didn't win."

"What?"

"You lost. I didn't have to do a thing."

"When a judge is in a shit mood," said Becker, "it's out of my hands."

"Out of your hands," muttered Arthur. "Did you do *any* work on this case? Did you do any preparation at all?"

"Hey listen, Kirkland . . ."

"You spent forty-five minutes questioning a witness who should've taken up no more than five minutes. And you asked the wrong questions!"

"My questions are my own business, no one else's. I asked—"

"This isn't law school anymore," said Arthur. He became conscious that he was shouting. "You just let a guilty man walk out onto the street because of your total, complete incompetence!"

Becker looked at him strangely. "What are *you* pissed off for? You won!"

"No," said Arthur. "I won nothing. You gave it to me, gift-wrapped."

"Roll of the dice," said Becker.

"It's not a game!" shouted Arthur. He was aware that he shouldn't be doing what he was doing. As a defense attorney, 90 percent of the people he represented were guilty, and sometime, somewhere, Becker would be prosecuting some of them. Deals would have to be made, deals that were the best Arthur could get for his clients, deals that depended as much on personal relationships as the letter of the law. What Arthur was doing now was not prudent, but he could not stop. "You know what I mean, Becker? It's not a game!"

"Go home, Kirkland," said Becker. He avoided Arthur's eyes.

"This whole thing here is supposed to have something to do with justice. And you've disgraced it."

Becker whirled round just in time to see Arthur stalk out.

6

JAY and Fresnell were waiting in the corridor.

"Congratulations," said Jay, matching strides with Arthur.

"For what?" said Arthur sullenly.

Fresnell steered him toward the men's room. "Come here," said Fresnell. "Come inside."

The three of them went through the door. Jay and Fresnell immediately fell to their knees and checked under the stalls for feet.

"Jesus," said Arthur, "this must be something. What are you looking for? Hidden microphones? Cameras?"

"You can't be too careful," said Jay.

"You can. It's called craziness."

"It's clear," said Fresnell, rising to his feet. He walked to Arthur, grinned, and put a meaty hand on his shoulder. "Judge Fleming!"

"Yeah?"

"I was right! He was arrested and booked this morning."

"Warren, that much we knew."

"But," said Jay gleefully, "you'll never guess what for!"

Fresnell began to laugh, his orange polka dot tie bouncing on his protruding belly. He walked to a sink, bent over, and splashed water on his face. Jay began to squeal.

"What?" said Arthur, grinning, "tell me!"

"You'll die!" choked Jay.

"Tell me!"

"Rrr—rrr—" Jay's hands gestured wildly. At the sink, Fresnell was doubled over in a paroxysm of laughter. "Rape!" gasped Jay finally.

Arthur's grin widened. "You mean—"

"Fleming was booked on a rape!"

Fresnell gripped the edges of the sink as his body shook with mirth. "I can't stand it! I can't stand it! Can you believe? Can you really . . ."

"Is that the best?" said Jay. "Tell me, is that the best?"

"Rape!" said Fresnell, his voice a high-pitched screech. A moment later he began to gag.

"I don't believe it," said Arthur, still smiling.

"But that's not even the best," choked Fresnell. Helplessly quivering, he turned to Jay. "Tell him," he said, tears streaming down his cheeks. "Tell him the punch line."

Jay had gotten back a modicum of control. "You're going to love this. His people just called the office."

"Whose?" said Arthur. "Fleming's?"

Jay nodded. "He wants *you* to represent him."

Fresnell, managing to straighten up, stared at Arthur expectantly. Jay, too, stood frozen, awaiting his partner's reaction. Arthur could not quite make sense out of what he had just been told. "Me?"

Fresnell collapsed on the floor this time, his pear-shaped body convulsing like a walrus being electrocuted.

Arthur raised his eyebrows. "Me?"

The second "me" severed the last vestiges of Porter's self-control. He stumbled into one of the stalls, shut the door and started banging on it. His cackling was wild. "It's so insane!" Jay shrieked. "Oh, my God, I am going to die, it is *so* insane!"

The metallic banging lasted for quite some time.

On the way to his meeting with Judge Fleming, Arthur stopped by the desk in the lock-up area. "Is Ralph Agee out yet?"

The desk clerk lowered his bifocals and ran his fingers down a list in front of him. "Agee, Agee . . . that the queen?"

"Yeah."

The clerk's finger stopped. He looked up. "He's out."

Arthur nodded and moved on.

Judge Henry Fleming was leaning on a metal table in the interrogation room. His lawyer, a bearded man named Marvin Bates, was seated, his closed attaché case in front of him. Arthur stood just inside the door.

"You're late," said Fleming. He brushed some imaginary dust off his sport jacket. "We were just about to leave."

"So leave," said Arthur.

Fleming's face went rigid. "Let's take this opportunity to get one thing straight. I hate your guts."

Arthur shrugged. "Well, I think you're a prick, but I don't have to go out of my way to tell you that." With Fleming, he knew, there could be no quarter. It was wholesale war, had been from the beginning.

"Mr. Kirkland," intoned Bates, "Judge Fleming has been accused—falsely, I might add—of sexually assaulting a young lady." He paused, seemed slightly surprised when Arthur offered no reaction. "He wants you to represent him in this case."

Arthur kept his gaze on Fleming. "Me represent you?"

Fleming nodded almost imperceptibly.

"Do you know how crazy that sounds?"

"Not really," said Fleming.

"Well, there are two lawyers up in the third floor men's room who think differently," said Arthur. "One of them is laughing so hard he's choking to death in the sink."

Again, Fleming dipped his head, as if men choking in the toilet were a natural consequence of his selection of a lawyer. "I am aware," he said slowly, "that I am not well liked."

"There are throngs cheering in the streets," said Arthur.

"And I am certain that there are many people who will be delighted when they hear about this." He pointed an expertly manicured index finger at Arthur's chest. "But the fact remains, I am innocent . . . and I fully intend to have this proven in a court of law."

"Best of luck," said Arthur. "At least you'll have the advantage at your trial that you won't be on the bench."

Determinedly, Fleming ignored him, but his concern was apparent. "Mr. Bates and I feel that, in this particular situation, you would be the perfect lawyer for my defense."

Arthur smiled. "Isn't that nice. What a wonderful compliment. And I thought I wasn't worthy . . ."

"Save the sarcasm, Kirkland."

"Right," said Arthur. "Okay. So the two of you put your little heads together and came up with me. That's wonderful. Now, the real question is why."

"Let's not be modest, Arthur," said Bates. "You've got a good reputation. You fight for what you believe in."

"So do a hundred others," said Arthur. He paused and glanced away. "Or at least a dozen."

"Yes," said Bates, "but your particular dislike for Judge Fleming is widely known. Defending him therefore lends a great deal of credibility to his case."

Arthur squinted. "Wait a minute. You mean you chose me because everyone would know I hate my client?"

Bates's eyes widened. "Precisely! Why else would you defend a man you dislike so much, unless he was truly innocent?"

Fleming advanced toward Arthur. "And I am, you know. I truly am."

"I don't give a shit," said Arthur. He turned to leave and found himself suddenly slammed against the door. Arthur twisted his head, caught sight of Fleming's face, red and furious. Arthur, surprisingly, felt unnaturally calm.

"You smug son of a bitch!" rasped Fleming.

"Uh, Henry," called Bates from the table. "Henry, I think you better let—"

"Shut up!" said Fleming, but he gradually eased the pressure on Arthur's waist.

Arthur felt his feet touch the floor and Fleming's hands withdraw. He stretched a bit, then turned around. Absurdly, all he could think to say was, "Thank you."

Fleming's eyes were smoldering. "I have never in my life committed a crime!" he said with quiet intensity.

Arthur returned the stare. "If you're really innocent, then I'm sorry for you." He shook his head. "But I won't defend you."

Daniel's was one of those knotty-pine-paneled, at-mospheric restaurants that use dim lighting, fake sty-rofoam wooden beams, and red-leather semicircular booths to distract attention from a fundamental medi-ocrity in food and service. Arthur and Gail Packer were slowly gnawing their way through fatty sirloin steaks when the waiter approached their table.

". . . and I was happily married with two terrific children," Gail was saying. "We were a couple out of a textbook, or at least so everyone thought."

"More water?" asked the waiter.

"Please," said Arthur. (For most of his adult life he had answered yes or no to this question, but re-cently he had heard people saying "Please" and thought he would try it. He realized now, however, that the sound of it—a kind of phony European so-phistication—was not for him.)

The waiter refilled their glasses.

"But Stephen thought that I wasn't dependent enough on him," Gail continued.

Arthur drained half his glass and the waiter, who hadn't left, began to fill it again.

"Uh, no," said Arthur, putting his hand over the glass. "I like to see it empty before adding new wa-ter. It gives me a sense of completion."

The waiter hesitated uncertainly.

"No more right now," said Arthur.

The waiter nodded curtly and left.

"I thought he was going to pour it between your fingers," said Gail. "Were you serious about that 'sense of completion' business?"

"Yes," said Arthur. "That's the way I am. I'm very organized. I eat everything on my plate, good or bad."

Gail narrowed her eyes. "You're crazier than you first appear."

"Thank you," said Arthur. "Anyway, getting back to you—your husband found you insufficiently de-pendent. Is that the same as 'too independent'?"

"I'm not quite sure *what* he meant," said Gail. She

paused a moment to remove some chive from her sour-cream-topped baked potato. "Actually I am, but . . . anyway, we went to a marriage counselor to try and figure things out."

"A shrink?"

"Yes." She raised her eyebrows. "Ever try one?"

"Once," said Arthur. "For about a month. He told me I was too aggressive. I said, 'you're right' and left." He speared a string bean. "But I think they're okay for some people."

"The one we went to was pretty good," said Gail. "After about five sessions, Stephen started to understand the source of our trouble and feel better about the relationship. He realized that I was his wife, not a competitor, and that his feelings of inferiority were inconsistent with his actual accomplishments. His ego really began to get stronger. It was amazing. I could see the transformation occurring right in front of me."

Arthur didn't look up. "And you?"

"Me, what?"

"Were you transformed also?"

"I started to feel worse," said Gail. Arthur raised his eyes and watched her as she picked a mushroom off the steak.

"You're a very finicky eater," he said.

"It's the lighting," said Gail sheepishly. "I like to see what I'm eating. If it were up to me I'd have them put spotlights on the plates. I like to do everything in the light."

"Everything?" said Arthur, grinning.

Gail nodded.

"I'll remember that. All right, I'm sorry—back to you feeling worse."

"I found," said Gail, "that all those years I hadn't been really happy at all. It's a paradox. If you're miserable but don't know it, you think you're happy . . . so maybe you are. But, of course, in reality you're not."

"But you became happy when you found out you were miserable?"

"Yes, because I realized my life was a sham." She picked a dust speck out of her water glass. "I was going through the motions of being a mother and a wife, but meanwhile sending subconscious messages that I wanted out."

"So Stephen wasn't crazy after all," said Arthur.

"Not entirely," said Gail. "These games always take two to play. Anyway, by the time he was ready for a second honeymoon, I was ready for a divorce. He was crying the night we separated."

"And you?"

"I cried for a lot longer. He comes every Wednesday to see the kids; I make sure I'm out. I enrolled in law school three months after we split up. I got sitters, went four nights a week."

"Nights are rough."

"Took me five years. Fortunately, I had a Bachelor's degree when I started. Otherwise you'd be talking to a crone."

Arthur smiled. "Why law?"

"I watched the guy who handled our divorce," said Gail. "It looked easy." She grinned. "Besides, there are too many teachers and typists in the world. It was either law or engineering, and I used to run straight D's in physics."

"So law was the path of least resistance."

Gail shrugged. "Wasn't it?"

"I hated law school," said Arthur. "I remember what they told us at orientation: 'Look at the man on your right, and now look at the man on your left. One of them won't be there when you graduate.' It was like being in a cancer ward."

"And was the prediction correct?"

"No," said Arthur.

"You mean both men made it through?"

"I mean neither made it through," said Arthur.

After dinner they went bowling at a nearby alley.

Arthur bowled a 116, 134, and 108, while Gail finished above 150 for all three games. Whereas Arthur's
ball hooked drastically and unpredictably, Gail threw
a perfectly controlled straight ball every time. Arthur
got occasional spectacular strikes, Gail quietly accum-
ulated spares. Arthur became frustrated and a bit
cranky, Gail remained calm. The only aspect of the
game they shared was an appreciation of each other's
behinds as they bent to release the ball.

"You're pretty good," said Arthur, when they'd
finished.

Gail shook her head. "Steady," she said. "But not
good. If you practiced as much as I do, you'd be
terrific."

"I have trouble controlling my release," said Arthur.

Gail grinned.

"I meant," explained Arthur, "I have weak wrists.
Everything else is fine."

They picked up some egg rolls and fried rice on
the way back to his apartment. Gail held the bag
while Arthur opened the door and switched on the
light. She slowly surveyed the living room as Arthur
headed toward the kitchen.

"You take renting an unfurnished apartment quite
literally, don't you? You know, it doesn't mean it has
to *stay* that way."

"I don't want to disturb it for the next owner,"
said Arthur over his shoulder.

Gail followed him into the kitchen.

"You put the food out," said Arthur. "I'll get some
plates."

He brushed past her on the way to the cupboard,
got a close whiff of musky perfume mixed faintly with
perspiration. Her eyes were very large and soft. The
cupboard contained only cereal boxes, half of them
opened. He tried another cabinet. Canned goods. If
I'm so organized, thought Arthur, how come I can't
find anything?

"Did you feel the knives in your back when you

75

walked out on the committee this morning?" asked Gail.

Arthur took down two plates from the third cabinet. "Yes, I did." He set the plates on the small kitchen table.

"Your comments caused quite a stir."

"That's a very dangerous group there," said Arthur.

"Why dangerous?" She placed an egg roll on each plate and opened the container of fried rice.

"Because you're conning the public into thinking you're doing something."

"But we are doing something," said Gail. "Got any forks?"

Arthur removed two forks from a drawer. "No. No, you're not. Care for some wine?"

Gail nodded.

"You're just skimming the surface," said Arthur. "You won't go after the real power." He opened the refrigerator and peered inside for several seconds before turning sheepishly around. "I, uh, don't have any wine. How about soda?"

Gail shook her head no. "What 'real power'?"

Arthur raised his eyebrows in a theatrical gesture of chagrin. "Now we know they're *definitely* safe." He closed the refrigerator door, moved to the sink and filled a glass with cold water.

"It seems to me that whenever I see you," said Gail, "you're always drinking water."

"Only drink you can trust," said Arthur. "All the others have preservatives, food colorings, carcinogens. . . ."

"What makes you such an authority on everything?"

"I'm not," said Arthur. "I don't pretend to be. It's just that in your case—I mean, in your committee's case—I don't think that the collective you knows what you're doing." He took out two candles from a cabinet, lit them on the stove, and placed them in glasses on the counter. Then he turned off the kitchen light and sat down next to Gail at the table.

"And I don't think you know your ass from a hole in the wall," said Gail.

The candles gave the room a warm orange glow.

"This is nice," said Arthur, "don't you think?"

"I'm angry again," said Gail. She bit off the end of her egg roll.

Gail pressed her lips together to keep from smiling. "I hate being angry. How can you criticize me for what I do? I don't spend nights in jail on contempt of court."

"Do you know what that's about?"

"Not really. It certainly doesn't seem consistent for a man who feels that everything is fixed and all attempts at reform are futile."

"That's not really my position," said Arthur. "It's just that things have a way of getting polarized in these . . . discussions."

"All right," said Gail, "then why the contempt?"

"I have a client," said Arthur, "who's in prison on account of a faulty taillight, and I can't get him out."

Gail wrinkled her brow. "What?"

Arthur nodded. "True. Let me tell you a little story about our wonderful judicial system. There's a guy named Jeff McCullaugh. He's driving down the highway one night and the police stop him for a faulty taillight. They run a make on him and the computer kicks back that a Jeff McCullaugh has an outstanding warrant in Alabama for assault with a deadly weapon."

"Is this the same Jeff McCullaugh?" Gail spread the innards of the egg roll meticulously over her plate.

"No. But he fit the general description," said Arthur. "So they arrest him." He helped himself to more rice. "Bail is set at five thousand dollars. Of course, he can't pay it, so he's sent to jail."

"What about a bondsman?"

"No good. McCullaugh doesn't own property, can't get a cosigner on a bond. They won't touch him."

Gail squinted carefully at the dismembered egg roll. She gingerly poked at several pieces with her fork.

"Then they appoint him a public defender," said Arthur, "and, of course, he's like all the rest of those guys. At the arraignment he makes a motion for a reduction of bail. The motion is denied. The next thing Jeff knows, a trial date is set six months away. The PD was so swamped with cases, that was his first open date. Jeff can't even contact the guy; he's never in his office, doesn't return calls." Arthur paused. "Did you ever consider a career in autopsies?"

Gail ignored him. "Didn't McCullaugh tell them they had the wrong person?"

"He tried," said Arthur. "But the PDs aren't set up to do investigations. They're oriented mainly toward getting their clients to plead guilty and then making deals. They simply haven't the time, in most cases, to prepare a defense or go to trial."

Gail seemed incredulous. "Are you— You're not serious, I mean—"

"Wait. It gets better. While Jeff is sitting in jail waiting for his trial, a prison guard is stabbed and the knife is planted in Jeff's cell." Arthur stood up. "I'm putting on the light. I can't stand what you're doing to that egg roll." He rose, crossed to the wall and flicked the switch.

"Sorry," said Gail. "It's just hard to sustain a romantic mood when I think of what might be inside that flaky little shell. I'm sorry, go on."

Arthur returned to the table. "So now McCullaugh is brought back to court on a new charge. Assault with a deadly weapon on a guard. The judge sets a new trial date *eleven* months from the date Jeff was first arrested."

"Which is not only unfair but unconstitutional."

"But, unfortunately," said Arthur, "not uncommon. Okay. Eleven months pass. A very frightened, sickly Jeff McCullaugh finally goes to trial. The public defender promises him that he can make a deal with the

78

judge: If McCullaugh pleads guilty, his sentence is limited to time already served."

Gail began eating discrete pieces of shrimp and bamboo shoots. "So he pleads guilty even though he's innocent."

"Right," said Arthur. "He figures it's worth it, he can go home right after the trial. Now, the deal was made with Judge Callahan, and the DA promises to maneuver the court calendar so he's presiding at the trial. But the day Jeff walks into court, Fleming is sitting on the bench. The DA tells Jeff's lawyer not to worry, Jeff pleads guilty, and Fleming sentences him to five years in state prison."

"Didn't Jeff try to change his plea?"

"Of course. Fleming refused."

Gail exhaled, shook her head.

"So," continued Arthur, "a little guy has spent two and one-half years in prison for a faulty taillight. I've spent one year getting enough evidence to get him out, and now Fleming refuses to reopen the case because it came in a few days late."

Gail pushed away her plate. "My God, that's really a horror story."

"Yeah," said Arthur. "Well, that's Judge Fleming for you."

"You can't fault him legally," said Gail. She saw Arthur wince. "He's going by the letter of the law."

Arthur held out his hand. "Please. Don't say those things. It'll start a fight and then you'll never get me into bed."

Gail smiled.

In the bedroom, Arthur kissed Gail on the lips. They were warm, incredibly soft. "There's the bathroom," he pointed, "if you want to get undressed."

"Right here is fine," she said.

"You don't mind if I watch?"

"Not as long as you get undressed too. That way we can both watch."

"Everything in the light," said Arthur, unbuttoning his shirt. "Don't think I didn't remember."

Gail unzipped her dress, pulled it over her head, and tossed it on a chair. Arthur removed his trousers. Gail came up to him and turned her back. "Want to help me unhook?" she said, indicating her bra.

"I'll try," said Arthur, "but I was never terrific at these things. At times like these, I'm all thumbs."

He felt her back, nestling against him, her curves nicely fitting his body. He dropped her bra, slid his arms around her, and cupped her lovely breasts. Delighted with her smell, her feel, he gently nudged her toward the bed.

"Look," said Arthur, breathing rapidly now. "I have to tell you . . . I've . . . it's been a while so I may not . . ."

"Me, too," said Gail, kissing his neck, his ear, his shoulder. "Counselor," she whispered, "I move we stop talking and just let it happen."

"Motion granted," said Arthur, reaching for her panties. "Mmm, Jesus, I'll grant anything. . . ."

Lying in bed sometime later, Gail stirred Arthur from his peaceful sleep with her giggling.

"What? What's so funny?" Arthur mumbled.

"I hate to tell you this," said Gail with an impish air, "but you remind me of my ex-husband."

"Why?"

"During sex, he was always yelling, 'Go, go, go,'" Gail said through her giggles.

"I don't know what's so funny," interrupted Arthur. "I don't say 'Go, go, go.'"

"Yes, you do."

"No. I say, 'God. God, God, God.'" Arthur, too, was now laughing.

"You sure it wasn't 'Go?'"

"Yes, I'm sure. That's a dumb thing to say—'Go.' I say 'God.' I always say 'God!'" At this, Arthur burst out laughing. Gail joined him in hysterics and as they were rolling around, laughing and giggling, there was a loud banging that startled them both.

"What the hell is that?" he said.

The hammering continued.

"It's the front door," said Gail, sitting up. Her eyes widened. "Arthur . . ."

Arthur forced himself to stand up. He grabbed a robe, wrapped it around his waist, and headed for the living room and the front door. "Yeah!" he called loudly, irritated by the intrusion. "Who is it!"

"Arthur?" came the voice. "It's Jay."

Arthur quickly unlocked the door and opened it. The stench of alcohol mixed with vomit was nearly overpowering. Jay sagged against one of the door jambs, righted himself, and walked uncertainly inside, past an astonished Arthur. Never before had he seen Jay drunk.

"Whaddaya say?" asked Jay.

Arthur closed the door and stood staring at his partner.

"Helluva night tonight," said Jay.

"You know it's two o'clock in the morning?"

"Of course I know," said Jay thickly. "The bars just closed."

"What are you doing here?" asked Arthur.

Jay's head moved back and forth. "Come to ask you a question," he said dully.

Arthur waited but Jay said nothing further. "What?" said Arthur finally.

"What?" said Jay.

"Jay, you said you came here to ask me a question."

"I did?"

"Yes."

"I think I forgot it."

"Jay, ma—"

"Oh, wait . . . wait. Here. Am I a good lawyer?"

Arthur looked at him blankly.

"That's the question," said Jay. *"Am I a good lawyer?"*

"Yeah, yeah," said Arthur reassuringly. "You're a terrific lawyer."

Jay wandered toward the back of the living room. "I got John Simms off. Right?"

"What are you talking about?"

"John Simms. John Simms. Killed his wife with a car. Drug dealer."

"Oh, right. Yeah," Arthur said. He remembered: the case with a million motions. "Yeah, you got him off."

"Not just 'got him off,' " said Jay. "Got him off on a murder. He was a murderer. We all know he did it. Everyone knew."

"That's right, Jay. We all know he was guilty."

Jay smiled and closed his eyes. He leaned heavily against a wall. "Brilliant. Brilliant defense."

"It was brilliant," said Arthur. The surprise of Jay's visit was beginning to wear off, and Arthur was rapidly becoming annoyed. Some nerve, he thought, coming here at this time, especially tonight, on some kind of drunken ego trip.

"Got him off on a technicality!" said Jay.

"Yeah, good. I know that."

"A technicality!" said Jay. He began a low, rumbling chuckle. "Reduced charges to manslaughter. Plea bargain for time served. And just like that"—he tried to snap his fingers, but missed—"home for lunch."

"Very nice" said. Arthur. "Look, Jay, why—"

"He did it again," said Jay.

Arthur's face dropped. "What?"

Jay nodded rapidly. "Simms. He did it again."

"What are you talking about?"

Jay looked up, his face a contorted mask of anguish. "About eleven, eleven-thirty tonight, he shot and killed his ex-wife's two kids." His voice broke. "I mean . . . kids."

Arthur felt the blood drain from his head. "Jesus," he whispered.

The two men looked at each other for several seconds, neither knowing what to say. "I gotta take a piss," muttered Jay finally. He brushed past Arthur toward the bedroom.

Inside, Gail was sitting on the bed, covers pulled up to her chin.

"Excuse me," said Jay politely. "I'm just going to take a piss."

Gail nodded and waved, as if this were a perfectly normal occurrence, night watchman bidding good evening to an office worker departing late. Jay disappeared into the bathroom as Arthur entered the bedroom.

"My partner," explained Arthur.

"He shares your bathroom?" said Gail.

Suddenly, there was a loud crash from behind the door. The sound of splintering glass seemed to linger in the air.

"Jay?" called Arthur.

No answer.

Arthur turned the bathroom doorknob, tried to open the door. There was a crack of light, just enough to see Jay's prostrate body, wedging the door shut. Arthur applied a careful, steady pressure, finally managed to squeeze himself inside. Jay struggled feebly to rise. "I think I slipped," he said.

Arthur put his hands under Jay's armpits and yanked upward. Jay rose two inches, then fell back. Arthur braced himself against the toilet bowl, careful to avoid the shards of broken glass that littered the tile floor. He again heaved Jay upward, managing somehow to raise him to a half-sitting position.

"You lost your robe," said Jay.

Arthur looked down at his robe near the base of the sink. It was wet.

"Did you pee on the floor?" asked Arthur, as if he were talking to an infant.

"I'm not sure," said Jay. "I peed on something."

"Probably on the floor," said Arthur. "And then you slipped on it. That would do it."

"That would do it," agreed Jay.

"Here," Arthur said. "Hold on to me." He reached out with his foot, and pulled the bathroom door open.

Gail, wearing her coat, was standing just outside. "Let me give you a hand."

"Stay out!" ordered Arthur. "There's glass all over!"

Gail backed away.

'Okay, Jay," said Arthur, "come on." He stood up and tugged Jay to his feet, then guided him out the door and toward the bed.

"Simms had his rights," said Jay, "and I protected those rights. Right?"

"You did fine," said Arthur. "Another two feet and you're there."

"Of course, the woman he killed also had rights, but that's not my concern. Right?"

Arthur turned Jay just as he got to the bed, maneuvered him into a sitting position.

"Rights is right," said Jay. "Or am I wrong?"

"Get me a washcloth," said Arthur to Gail. "Watch the glass."

She disappeared into the bathroom.

"Arthur," said Jay, his voice pleading, "am I responsible for those kids?"

Arthur, completely nude, grabbed Jay's legs. "You did fine," he said. "Here, put your feet up."

Jay leaned back against the headboard, his legs stretched out in front of him. Gail emerged from the bathroom with a wet washcloth and handed it to Arthur. "What's wrong?" she asked.

Arthur shook his head, motioned her to be silent.

"Arthur," moaned Jay. "I did what I was supposed to do, didn't I?"

"You did," said Arthur.

"So therefore . . . all's well."

"All is well," said Arthur. He unfolded the wash-cloth and placed it on Jay's forehead.

"Arthur, what's going on?" asked Gail.

Arthur turned. He was still lightheaded and shaken. "Two kids are dead," he said quietly. "He wants to know if he's an accomplice."

"I don't un—" began Gail, but stopped when she saw Arthur place a finger to his lips.

"Art," said Jay sluggishly, "I think I'm just going to take a little nap here. Couple minutes." His eyes closed. He turned his head slightly and the washcloth slipped to the pillow. Arthur gently placed it back in position on Jay's forehead.

Gail, feeling awkward and out of place, lingered near the foot of the bed. "Is there anything I can do?"

"No," said Arthur.

"Just a couple minutes," mumbled Jay.

"Shall I leave?" asked Gail.

"Yeah," said Arthur. "Please." He looked up at her. "I'm sorry."

Gail nodded and headed for the bathroom.

"Hey," said Arthur.

She stopped.

"I'll see you," he said.

7

HE felt as if he was on the inside of a food processor. He was being shaken to pieces, made into Cream-of-Arthur soup. He leaned over toward Rayford and shouted over the pulsing staccato of the huge, whirling blades. "I thought you flew . . . uh . . . you know . . . planes."

Judge Rayford smiled and pulled upward on the collective pitch lever with his left hand. Abruptly, the craft rose, sending Arthur's stomach careening earthward. "Nope," said Rayford crisply. "Been flying helicopters ever since Korea."

Arthur was amazed. He had gotten to the tiny, private airport at 10 A.M. and spotted Rayford immediately near one of the hangars. "What does this place use for runways," he had joked, "bicycle paths?"

Rayford had shrugged. "Doesn't matter to me," he'd said.

And then Arthur had seen it. A Kawasaki 369HS. "Used to be a sub-chaser," Rayford had explained. "Originally made by Hughes for the Spanish Navy. Military version, that is. I got it for a song." Arthur wondered how one went about getting things for songs from the Spanish Navy, but decided not to pursue it. Ten minutes later they had taken off, Arthur's face ash white, his body rigid.

Now, he decided it would be good to focus on not vomiting. He looked out of the glass bubble at the Maryland countryside dizzily receding below. Arthur tried to remember something he had heard about seasickness: To avoid nausea, look at a point on the horizon. Or maybe it was, Don't look at a point on the horizon. He had forgotten which. It didn't matter. He was too terrified to concentrate on anything. "I have to tell you, Frank," he gasped, "I'm not too happy about this. Couldn't we just hover."

Rayford smiled avuncularly. "Just relax, Arthur." He stepped on the right rudder pedal and the craft pivoted neatly on a vertical axis. "Here we go," said Rayford. He pushed forward on the cyclic-pitch stick between his knees, and the helicopter shot forward. Hump-backed hills clad in sweeping whorls of brilliant autumn colors rolled up under them. Arthur's stomach heaved.

"Pretty, isn't it?" said Rayford.

"I don't want to talk," choked Arthur.

Rayford raised his eyebrows. "You ever skydive?" Arthur shook his head.

"You should. You might learn something."

Arthur thought that he had already learned something right here, without the skydiving: Never trust your life to half-crazed strangers. Dishonor before death.

"I was skydiving one day," said Rayford, "and my main chute didn't open. I pulled the ripcord on my backup chute, and that one didn't open either. It was jammed." He twisted the throttle grip on the end of the collective-pitch lever and a spasm of vibration shot through the cabin.

"Nnn," said Arthur.

"Don't worry about that," said Rayford. "Little tracking problem is all. Tip paths of the rotor blades don't all coincide. I can fix it in a minute on the ground."

Then why didn't you, thought Arthur.

"Anyway," said Rayford, "there I was, plunging to the earth at thirty-two feet per second squared, and just as I saw the treetops, I discovered the meaning of life."

"Which is?" said Arthur, sick but still curious.

"It sucks," said Rayford.

You don't need to almost die to learn that, thought Arthur. He wondered how Rayford had, in fact, survived, but decided not to ask. Perhaps the story had been apocryphal, a kind of fable from which to draw a moral, a Zen koan for the flying set.

"They used to keep Native Dancer down there," said Rayford.

Arthur carefully tilted his head down.

"You missed it," said the judge.

A moment later they were over Baltimore, surveying the wrecked, shattered area adjacent to the Inner Harbor.

"By the way," said Rayford, "the board voted to purchase the prison boat."

"That's good news," said Arthur, uncaring.

"Except we have to find another place to dock it. People from the Inner Harbor are drawing up a petition to have it relocated."

"Where to?"

"Anywhere but their neighborhood."

They moved inland.

"Sorry about Jay," said Rayford. "How's he taking the Simms thing?"

"Not too well, I think," said Arthur. Gradually, he was becoming less tense. He could conceive—although never in his particular case—how this type of flying might actually prove pleasurable to someone. "I can't get him to talk about it," he said.

"He'll be all right," said Rayford. "Hazards of the trade. Any business involves risk, that's why we have insurance companies. A good lawyer can get the guilty off, and a bad one can send the innocent to jail."

"You're missing the point," said Arthur. "How do you deal with it? Jay isn't able to."

"There is no way to deal with it," said Rayford.

"So what's the solution?"

"The solution is don't even try." Rayford studied

the control panel in front of him. A dozen needles quivered inside illuminated graticules. "Hey!" he said ebulliently. "We've hit it!"

"Hit what?"

Rayford just smiled.

"Hit what?" repeated Arthur more urgently. He didn't feel like hitting anything just then.

"The betting point," said Rayford. "It's a game I play. Each time I go out I calculate how much fuel I have and how far I can go on it and still get back."

Arthur closed his eyes, trying not to absorb the meaning of Rayford's words.

"Then," continued Rayford, "I figure out the half-way point and go a little beyond it."

"Don't tell me we're beyond the halfway point," pleaded Arthur.

"Yes!" said Rayford triumphantly. "But I won't tell you if you really don't want to know," he added quickly.

Arthur felt his heart rate rapidly accelerate. Major muscle groups in his body suddenly went limp. "You mean we're not going to make it back?" he asked, his voice quavering.

"Maybe," said Rayford pleasantly. "Maybe not."

I'm going to die, thought Arthur lucidly. "Land!" he yelled. "Put it down *now!*"

Rayford shook his head. Don't worry. We're not in trouble, yet."

Arthur wondered about his funeral. Who would bury him? Jay? Jay was already depressed, he didn't need any more trouble. And what would happen to his cases, to McCullaugh and Mrs. Patterson, to Ralph Agee, to Gibson—and to Fleming. What horrible luck, to miss the Fleming indictment! The unfairness, the irony . . .

"Okay," said Rayford cheerfully, turning the helicopter 180 degrees. "Here we go-o. Heading on back."

Arthur sat rigid as the ruined city passed beneath

them and they flashed out again into the countryside. Why this type of death, he wondered. Why not a heart attack, say? He was certainly the right type, excitable, on-the-go, tense. Or maybe a little cancer. True, the medical expenses would be a financial drain, but at least he could do some reading in the hospital, make small talk with the nurses, put things in perspective. With this crazy noise and vibration all around him, how could he even think? It seemed to him that a great deal of time had gone by, and he began to steel himself for the crash. He had the impression Rayford was talking to him, telling him things, but he couldn't be sure. Final instructions perhaps (tuck your head between your knees, brace your arms, etc.), anecdotes, philosophical observations—it didn't matter now. No need to feign courtesy. He saw Rayford lean toward him.

"Sixteen years," said the judge.

If, thought Arthur, by some miracle I live through this (undoubtedly as a quadriplegic), I will never fly again. Never.

"Sixteen years of marriage and my wife won't eat Chinese food."

Arthur thought he recognized a group of hills in the distance, the swirls of color. . . .

"It's crazy," said Rayford.

Not a helicopter, not a plane, not even an elevator, thought Arthur. He made a silent deal with a God he didn't believe in: Get me out of this one—even maimed—and I'll never take an elevator again. I'll move to the ground floor. I won't even wear heels on my shoes.

"Especially since we met in a Chinese restaurant."

"How are we doing?" Arthur asked intensely.

"What?" yelled Rayford.

"Are we back yet?" snapped Arthur. "Where are we?"

"Arthur," said Rayford, "trust me. I know what I'm doing."

"You know what it really is," said Rayford. "It's a protest. See, she relates Chinese food to our marriage."

Arthur closed his eyes and spoke to himself. "We went too far. I know it. I did something against my best judgment and now I pay for it with my life. It's coming. I feel it. We went too far." He opened his eyes. In the distance he could see the airport.

"Look at that!" shouted Rayford. "You see it?"

"I see it!" said Arthur. In his mind, scenes from old movies: four emaciated, half-dead survivors on a rubber raft in the Pacific point upward to a circling rescue plane.

"I tell you," said Rayford. "I've got good instincts."

Suddenly, Arthur felt a sickening tug at his bowels. A moment later he heard the engine sputter uncertainly, then die. A pair of concentric instrument needles, formerly lined up, rapidly separated. "Oh, my God," whimpered Arthur. "Oh, God."

Rayford quickly jammed down the collective pitch lever to the bottom stop. The helicopter plummeted dizzily downward, blades flailing wildly at the air. "Hang on, Arthur!" Rayford made another adjustment and their forward speed decreased somewhat as their descent slowed. Arthur's teeth hurt from being clenched so tightly. His neck muscles were taut as guitar strings. Fifteen feet above the ground, the aircraft seemed to pause, as if deciding whether to kill them, then settled gently onto the grass. Slowly, the rotor came to a halt.

"Home free!" said Rayford excitedly. "Autorotation. That's what makes these damn things so safe. Even if you run out of fuel, the air currents always keep the rotor going so you can get down. Course, you gotta know how, and sometimes you can't land, and sometimes it's too late and you crash, but—" He peered out the Plexiglas canopy. They had landed in some tall weeds, fifty yards from the airport, missing a high-voltage power line by three feet. "Home free!"

repeated Rayford. He turned to Arthur. "You all right?"

Arthur sat rigid, his eyes bulging open.

"We almost made it right on the button," said Rayford. "I told you I had good instincts."

Arthur, unable to speak, the words not registering on his mind, did not so much as blink.

A half-hour later, he and Rayford were seated in the airport coffee shop, looking out at the runways. Arthur's hand trembled as he carefully lifted a steaming cup to his lips. Rayford smiled condescendingly.

"You'll be all right. Your adrenalin's still charged. But you've got to admit, it makes you feel alive, vital." Rayford bit into a chicken salad on rye.

"It makes me feel something. But I don't know if alive and vital aptly describe it," contradicted Arthur. "I don't know about you, but I could be dead right now, or worse."

Rayford scoffed. "Why does everyone have such a morbid preoccupation with death?"

"I'm not always preoccupied with it," said Arthur. "But this certainly seems like a valid time."

"Oh, don't be melodramatic."

A waitress came to the table and tried to refill their coffee cups. "I'll wait till I finish this one," said Arthur.

"I'd like another chicken-salad sandwich when you get a chance," said Rayford.

"You haven't even finished this one," said Arthur.

"I'm looking ahead," said Rayford. "Did you want anything, by the way?"

Arthur held up his palm. "My stomach is still in suspended animation."

The waitress left.

"Speaking of looking ahead," said Rayford, "I understand you won't even consider taking on Fleming's case."

"That's right," said Arthur.

"I don't understand why you're so adamant," said Rayford. "Put aside your personal feelings, for Chrissake. The man needs help."

"You think he's innocent?"

Rayford nodded. "I know Fleming. He screws around a lot, but he's no rapist."

Arthur considered: Defending Fleming would give him incredible prestige in the legal community, not to mention the extravagant publicity. The case would be front-page news in all the papers. It was tawdry and sensational. Win or lose, the exposure meant that Arthur could probably double his income in the next year. Take in another partner. Move to better offices. He had defended people whom he knew were guilty, so why not Fleming? The answer came to him even before he had finished forming the question. It was remarkable in its clarity: He hated the man, hated him personally and professionally. He remembered a book he had read years ago, *The Magic Christian*. It was about a man of limitless wealth who conducted experiments on people to prove that a sufficient amount of money could buy any disgusting, perverted act the rich man could think of. Well, not me, thought Arthur, not me. "Every time I see him presiding over a case," he said, "it pisses me off."

"A lot of us were bad," said Rayford. "If you can't make it as a lawyer, becoming a judge is a perfect move. I was a terrible lawyer. I used to come to court three hours late, borrow money from my clients."

Arthur smiled.

"Yeah, true. I used to put my clients in different rooms in my office, make them wait tremendous amounts of time. I would look in every half-hour, ask how they were, and leave before they could answer. I was miserable, a nervous wreck. I got hooked on Gothic novels, I still read two or three a day. I was falling apart—and then I became a judge. All the years of politics finally paid off." He paused. "I'm not a great judge, Arthur. . . ."

"You're fine."

"Competent. I am competent. I try. I study the law. I attempt to be fair." He licked his lips. "Fleming's not the best, true, but he isn't the worst either. Not many of his decisions are reversed on appeal; that counts for something. As far as you and he go, I dunno, you two can never seem to agree."

Arthur finished his coffee. "Tell him no, I'm sorry. You tried your best."

"You're a tough man, Arthur."

"I wish," said Arthur. He remembered years ago, his first case. The DA and Rayford had both exerted heavy pressure on him to make a deal. The court calendar was overflowing; Arthur's client was unsympathetic, the evidence against him appeared conclusive. The DA offered to reduce the four charges to one; Rayford would limit the sentence to a maximum of one year. Young, inexperienced, and alone (it was before he'd met Jay), Arthur had refused the deal. Rayford and the DA were furious. They had hammered at him, badgered him, threatened. Arthur had stood firm. Six months later, at the trial, he had demolished the prosecution's chief witness. The jury voted to acquit on all charges. Afterward, Rayford had called Arthur into chambers. "You were foolish to refuse that deal," he had said. "But you were right. I admire your guts." He then invited Arthur out for a drink; it had been the beginning of a relationship based on mutual respect, if not friendship.

"God," said Rayford now, "I hate being a go-between."

"It's like getting people blind dates," said Arthur. "I don't think you can win. Anyway, it's over."

The waitress returned with Rayford's chicken-salad sandwich. Outside, Arthur could see men hauling Rayford's helicopter into the hangar.

"It's not all over," said Rayford, eyes riveted on his plate. "Arthur . . . there are some people in this town who can ruin your career if you refuse."

"What do you mean, 'ruin my career'?" said Arthur. He was irritated, a sign the effects of the helicopter ride had worn off.

"They can have you disbarred."

"For what? Contempt of court? Hundreds of—"

"Not contempt of court."

"Then what?"

"They . . . someone did a little digging." Rayford shook his head. "God, I hate this. . . ."

"Tell me," said Arthur. "I'd rather hear it from you than read it in the papers."

Rayford took a deep breath. "Someone found out that you violated the lawyer-client confidentiality principle one time."

"What? That's—When?"

"Did you ever have a client by the name of Ernest Drago?"

Arthur tensed. Oh, Christ, he thought, not that. "Yes."

"You gave information to the police on the q.t. that led to his arrest and conviction."

Arthur nodded slowly. "Are you familiar with the case?"

"Slightly."

"Drago was insane. I handled him on a burglary charge. He'd only done it once . . . to fulfill what he called his 'fantasy trips.' The guy had spent half his life in mental hospitals. The police would find him wandering the streets, naked. He thought he was invulnerable, the messiah. He heard voices that told him what to do. He'd sit in my office and rattle off the most grotesque ideas you can imagine. Hacking people's fingers off, digit by digit. Putting needles through their eyes. One of his things was wondering what would happen if you put a firecracker in someone's mouth. That was one of his favorites."

"And he was out on the streets."

"Yes. Frightening, isn't it? Anyway, one day I read in the papers that a couple of people had almost been killed by somebody holding them up with a gun and forcing cherry bombs in their mouths. A fourteen-year-old girl had the left side of her face blown off." Arthur slapped the table. "I knew it was Drago, so I told the police."

Rayford wiped some chicken salad from the corner ner of his mouth. "The specifics don't make any difference."

"That's crazy. The specifics are the crucial difference."

"You violated the Code of Ethics and they can have you disbarred. Not to mention all this other shit you've been getting into lately."

Arthur stared at the ceiling in frustration. "You know, I can't believe this. I can't believe what I'm hearing. This is so insane I'd never accept it if I wasn't right in the middle. Tell me, back in the helicopter there, did we actually crash, maybe, and go through the looking glass? Really, I'd like to know—what the hell is going on?"

"Don't despair," said Rayford.

"Who's despairing?"

"The fact remains you are a very principled, ethical lawyer with no political ties. The perfect candidate to represent Fleming."

"That's wonderful," said Arthur. "They want me to defend this man because of my moral integrity, or else they'll disbar me for being unethical."

Rayford nodded.

"Support mental health or I'll kill you," said Arthur. "That's what you're telling me, right?"

For the first time Rayford's expression was pained. Arthur knew it was a look that rarely surfaced in this man. "I don't want to see you get hurt, Arthur," said Rayford softly. His words were measured. "Take the case. Don't throw away your whole career."

Arthur stared out the window. "Jesus," he muttered. "I don't believe this." He thought: It would not be the worst thing I've ever done. There are better issues to take moral stands on. He turned back to Rayford. "Will Fleming take a polygraph?"

"I don't know."

"Well, how do I find out?"

"Ask him. Make an appointment and ask him." He paused. "Does this mean you'll consider taking the case?"

"I don't know," said Arthur thoughtfully. "I honestly don't know."

8

FLEMING sat back in his green leather chair and pressed a button on the squat slide projector that rested on his desk. There was a clicking sound and then a hum, and abruptly a picture of a vase materialized on the white paneled door to his office. Fleming studied the image appreciatively. The vase was French, nineteenth century, in the neoclassical Louis XVI Empire style. It had been made in Sèvres of hardpaste porcelain, its decoration consisting of raised, filigreed gold surrounding a pictorial panel depicting a spring landscape. The colors—creamy whites, turquoises, cameo pinks, cobalt blues—were breathtaking. Fleming let his eyes drink in the beauty. Even though he was alone, there was a certain amount of self-consciousness to the gesture, a heightened awareness that never left him, that permeated his every thought and action. He was, after all, one of those people who'd been granted a special gift, the gift of aesthetic taste. He was a connoisseur—literally, one who knows; a connoisseur of art, of beauty, of fine foods, and wines. The fact that he was a judge, then, seemed only to follow a natural order: The same sense of keen discrimination that permitted him to distinguish fine art from shoddy functioned equally well for interpreting subtle points of law. What it came down to finally, he understood, was that society needed someone to set the standards of taste—someone to make educated, penetrating judgments—and he was such a person.

He pressed the switch again, but the projector's whirr was drowned out by the sudden buzz of the intercom. Fleming shook his head in annoyance, then leaned over the baffle of the small gray box. "What is it?" he asked tartly.

A female voice mechanized by integrated circuits: "Mr. Kirkland wanted to remind you that he's still waiting."

"I'm aware of that, Doris."

"Will you be very long, sir? He's been here over a half-hour."

Fleming sighed. "All right. I suppose you can send him in."

A moment later the door opened. Arthur stood immobilized in the polychromatic shafts of light. On his face was the image of a large earthenware container; a red-and-green flower fell across his nose, orange beads ringed his forehead, his ears were yellow and green handles.

"Come on in," said Fleming. "Close the door."

Arthur shielded his eyes, ducked down, and shut the door behind him. He moved several feet to the side to escape the projector's direct beam.

"Have a seat," said Fleming.

Arthur cautiously made his way across the room to a wooden chair on the other side of the desk.

"Know what that is?" said Fleming.

"A vase," said Arthur.

Fleming chuckled. "A mosque lamp," he said. "Turkish. Tin glazed in the sixteenth century."

Arthur heard a click and then a whirr; the room was dark.

"Do you like antiques?" came Fleming's voice.

"Only new ones," said Arthur.

A new slide appeared, a plate this time, painted in orange-gold with a blue background.

"I hope your line of defense is more successful than your humor," said Fleming.

Arthur stared straight ahead. "If you don't like it, you can get yourself another lawyer. I just like to hang around with my clients and tell jokes."

"Hold it," said Fleming, tearing himself away from the slide to glare at Arthur. "Let's clear the air for a second. I want you to know this up front. You're one of those self-righteous lawyers who wants to change the law to serve the needs of the individual. Well, that's a lot of bullshit, and I don't want it in my court."

Arthur swiveled to face him in the dim light. "Wait a minute! That so-called bullshit I gave you was new evidence proving beyond a doubt that McCullaugh is innocent."

"I understand that," said Fleming. "I read your brief very carefully."

"Well . . . ?"

"But the fact is it was not submitted within the allotted time."

"Three days late—"

"Not in the allotted time. Therefore, it is invalid, and the defendant remains guilty, even though he's innocent." Fleming reclined. This is what these lawyers simply could not get through their heads—that the law was like a perfectly tuned orchestra. Loosen one string on one instrument, and an entire concerto could be destroyed. Cacophony. The lawyers were concerned only with the sound of their particular strings; their minds lacked the breadth and power to encompass the entire symphony in its splendor.

"It doesn't bother you," said Arthur, "that a man

is going to serve nine years for something he didn't do?"

"It doesn't bother me because I'm following the law," said Fleming.

"That's insane!"

"It's the law!" Fleming pressed the switch on the projector. A green-and-white teapot appeared on the door. "Shino stoneware," he said. "Japan, Momoyama period, late-sixteenth, early-seventeenth century."

"I want you to see what you can do for McCullaugh," said Arthur.

"Nothing can be done," snapped Fleming.

"I don't buy that."

"I don't care what the hell you buy, mister. You don't do the pushing. You're in no position to push for anything." Change of slide: faïence jug from Talavera, Spain, medieval Paterna tradition, seventeenth century. Fleming inhaled. "Nevertheless . . . I'll see what I can do."

"That's a nice pot."

"Tin-glazed," said Fleming. "It's called faïence, after the town of Faeze in Italy, although this one is Spanish."

"You're very knowledgeable about this stuff."

"One of my hobbies. My own collection is rather meager; I spend most of my time mooning over these slides. I have slides of everything."

Arthur stared at the projector. "Tell me about Leah Shepard."

"What do you want to know?"

"How many times did you see her?"

"I saw her on two occasions. She works over at City Hall."

"Did you have sexual relations with her on the first date?" For just an instant, it seemed peculiar to Arthur that he should be talking to a distinguished, fiftyish man about dates and sexual relations. Of course, there was no reason why people shouldn't have either, even in their seventies or eighties, except . . .

"Yes, I did," said Fleming. "First and second dates. That's why this whole business makes no sense to me."

"What do you think happened to her?"

Fleming shook his head. "I assure you, I didn't rape her. I don't know. Maybe she's got an angry boyfriend who showed up after I left."

"'Angry' is a little mild," Arthur said. "The girl wasn't just raped. She was brutally beaten and sodomized. That goes way beyond angry."

The projector motor whirred. "Of course it does," said Fleming. "I'm sorry."

Arthur perked up. He hadn't expected any expression of sympathy whatsoever.

"But what the hell am I doing in this mess?" said Fleming. "I've been involved in law for over thirty years. Right now I can't find five people who want to believe I'm innocent. Not five!" He fired off two slides in rapid succession. "I may not win popularity contests, but there's no reason I should be crucified."

Arthur looked at him and nodded. "That's right, there isn't. Look, I want you to take a polygraph test."

"Why? It's not admissible as evidence."

"I want you to take it."

"I'll think about it."

"I want you to do it."

Fleming stood up. "I said"—his voice thundered —"I'll think about it!"

Arthur stood up also and moved toward the door. "Fine. And I'll think about taking your case." His hand closed on the doorknob.

"You don't have much choice," said Fleming ominously. He pressed the button on the projector.

Arthur stood illuminated by a Pennsylvania Dutch pie plate.

"U.S.A.," said Fleming. "Early eighteen hundreds."

Arthur closed the door behind him as he left.

After lunch he went down to the Y for an hour, worked out in the weight room, did ten laps in the pool, finally went up to the four-wall courts to see if he could get a game of racquetball. A lone figure was practicing against the front wall.

"Name's Manny," said the man, a beefy, red-faced fellow who wore a bandanna around his forehead.

Arthur asked him if he wanted to play racquetball, but the man just laughed.

"Sissy game," he said. "I play only handball. You see these?" He held up his palms. "Tough as nails. Like sandpaper."

"Come on," said Arthur, "I'll lend you a racquet."

"You use the racquet," said Manny. "I'll use my hands. And I'll tell you why you're gonna lose. With my hands I can put spins on the ball like you wouldn't believe. I can hook it and slice it. I can take balls in the corners your racquet can't get near." He paused. "Tell you what, I'll spot you five points."

"Okay," said Arthur pleasantly.

They began to play, Arthur not caring whether he won or lost as long as he ran, hit hard, worked up a sweat. He played fiercely and furiously; the small black ball ricocheted wildly around the walls, floor, and ceiling. The riflelike sounds echoed hollowly in the sealed enclosure. Arthur won the game twenty-one to three.

"What happened to your theory?" he asked afterward.

"It was a bluff," said the heavy-breathing Manny. "I tried to psych you out. My hands are killing me."

"Next time try using a racquet," said Arthur.

He stood in the anteroom near the secretary's desk and watched his partner through a crack in the door. Jay was standing with hands on hips, surveying his office. It was his expression that had first caught Arthur's attention, had stopped him from walking right in. There was something . . . *not right* about it. Jay walked over to his desk, picked up two pencils, sharpened them in the electric sharpener. Each time he withdrew them he somehow managed to break the points, until finally all that were left were nubs. Jay placed the nubs neatly back on the desk.

Once more, he surveyed the room. Strangely, the desk top was nearly empty. Arthur wondered how Jay had managed to dispose of the usual pile of paperwork. He saw Jay walk to the file cabinet, open a drawer, withdraw several folders . . . and strew them on the desk, seemingly at random. Again, Jay stood back, pondering. After a moment he crossed to the bookcase, took out four books, opened them, placed two on a couch and two on a chair. He opened up a desk drawer, tore six sheets off a lined yellow pad, crumpled them, and very carefully placed them in the trash can. Arthur shook his head.

When he saw Jay enter the bathroom, Arthur walked into the office. The bathroom door was partially open. He watched as Jay lifted up the toilet seat and checked the rim. Seconds later Jay was wiping the rim with toilet paper, not once but several times, flinging the used sheets into the bowl and, finally, flushing a huge wad. He saw Arthur when he turned.

"When you finish in here, Ethel," said Arthur, "would you mind doing mine?"

Jay grinned sheepishly.

"I have some tracing paper in my desk," said Arthur. "We could cut it into a long strip, letter SANITIZED FOR YOUR PROTECTION on it, and wrap it around the toilet seat. Would that make you feel better?"

"All right," said Jay. He stepped out of the bathroom and closed the light. "Don Welton is coming in, and I just wanted to clean up the place a little."

"The contractor?"

"That's right. I can't wait to get out of dealing with this low-end crap."

Welton was a multimillionaire builder of condominiums. He was being sued by several people who had bought units for investment purposes and then claimed the facilities were not as represented. The heated pool was freezing. The tennis court was a Ping-Pong table. The guard on duty twenty-four hours had apparently left after twenty-five. Welton had listened to the complaints sympathetically, then advised the people to sue him. For the law firm of Kirkland and Porter, Welton's patronage meant possible entrée into a world of very wealthy clients. The superrich were always being sued by those of lower economic status or suing one another. It was an absorbing way to pass the time, and it benefited the lawyers. The divorce rate of the wealthy was also twice as high as that for the rest of the population.

"What's with you and Fleming?" asked Jay.

"I'm going to take it," said Arthur.

"Good for you."

"He'll see what he can do about McCullaugh, and he agreed to take a polygraph."

"Very impressive," said Jay. "How'd you bluff him into it?"

"By not bluffing," said Arthur.

The intercom buzzed and Jay picked up the receiver. "Yes?"

"Mr. Welton is here," came Sherry's voice.

"I'll be right out," said Jay.

"Just tell me," said Arthur, "why did you put those files on your desk and crumple those papers in the garbage?"

"You saw that?"

"Yes."

"You were spying on me?"

"Yes."

"I wanted to make it seem like I had work, like I was busy. Nothing turns a client off faster than a lawyer who seems hungry."

"Why didn't you just leave your desk the way it was? What happened to the pile of papers you normally have?"

"Oh, those," said Jay. "I cleaned those off. Didn't want to seem overloaded and disorganized. Nothing turns a client off faster than a lawyer who seems too busy to give him sufficient time."

"Nothing except a bathroom toilet seat that isn't polished to a mirror shine," said Arthur.

"Don't tease," said Jay. "You have your quirks too, you know."

"But mine are reasonable quirks, yours are irrational."

Jay headed toward the door.

"Hey, what's this?" said Arthur, spotting a small golden statue on a bookcase shelf.

"I told Welton I was a golfer," said Jay, lowering his voice. "I told him I won trophies."

Arthur examined the statue more closely. "But this is for badminton. You think this is going to impress Welton?"

"It looks pretty good from a distance," said Jay defensively. "He's not going to actually read it."

"You're right," said Arthur. "He'll be too busy looking at his reflection in the toilet seat."

Arthur sat on one side of the heavy screen in the visitor's room and waited. Whenever he visited the Maryland Penitentiary, he felt an overwhelming sense of claustrophobia and confinement. There was something about the walls, the buff-colored bricks, the low ceiling, some subtle maladjustment of proportions that made him want to scream—and he was only a visitor. Imagine, he thought, if I was forced to stay here. . . .

A door on the back wall opened and Jeff McCullaugh, led by a guard, came into the room. He walked over to the screen opposite Arthur and sat down on a wooden chair. Two screens down, a black woman was speaking excitedly to a wiry black man. Arthur stared at McCullaugh's face. High on his right cheek a vein-streaked, purplish swelling had nearly closed one eye. His lips were puffy and bruised.

"What happened?" said Arthur.

"Somebody beat me up," said McCullaugh thickly.

"What for?"

"I didn't ask."

"Well, did you tell anybody?"

"Who?"

"I dunno . . . the guards, the warden . . . somebody?"

McCullaugh tried to laugh but his face simply could not accommodate the stretching.

"You want me to have someone look into it?" said Arthur. "Maybe we can—"

"No." McCullaugh leaned in. "Look, you've got to get me out of here."

"I'm trying," said Arthur. "Believe me. I think I'm getting close."

"I don't understand what's going on," said McCullaugh, his voice hoarse with desperation.

"I've talked to Judge Fleming," said Arthur, trying to keep his voice calm. "We're going to work something out." It would be easy to be caught up in the panic, to let himself get swept away. But it would be devastating for McCullaugh. The lawyer must always *appear* to have things under control.

"You gotta do something soon," McCullaugh pleaded. "Man, I seen some things here that are just genuine horror stories. You don't know what goes on here."

"I do know," said Arthur. "I know it's bad."

"Then get me out." McCullaugh placed his fingers on the screen. "Please . . ."

"Jeff . . . just try to take care of yourself for another three weeks; can you last three weeks?"

"I don't know. I really don't know."

"I promise I'll have you out by then. You have my word on it."

"I don't know," muttered McCullaugh. "I don't know." His eyes appeared feverish.

"If you can't make the three weeks, tell me now," said Arthur. "Maybe you could be shifted."

"I'm trying," said McCullaugh. "I'm trying to make it on my own. I got myself thrown into solitary just to get away from some guys."

Arthur nodded. He had seen men in solitary. The rooms were eight-foot cubes made of pale-gray concrete, windowless, a light kept on twenty-four hours a day. There was no bed. On the jail tours, when he'd looked into the cells, the prisoners would be hunched on the stone floor, their eyes burning with the ferocity of animals. . . .

"Christ," said McCullaugh, "if this don't beat all."

"Hang on," said Arthur.

"Read in the papers about lettin' all these people out of prison 'cause it's too crowded, and here I am."

"I'm going to get you out, Jeff."

McCullaugh seemed half-dazed. "If that don't beat all," he said. "If that don't beat all."

Arthur stopped by the bulletin board on his way into the home. At the top, in large multicolored letters, were the words HAPPY THANKSGIVING, and below were a series of childlike paintings depicting pilgrims, turkeys, ears of corn, etc. Next to the paintings was a large card inscribed A GIFT FROM THE MILFORD MILL ELEMENTARY SCHOOL. Below the card was a notice: NEXT TRIP, THURSDAY, DEC. 8—A DAY IN DICKEYVILLE! COME SEE THIS HISTORIC 18TH CENTURY INDUSTRIAL VILLAGE ON GWYNNS FALLS. THIS CHARMING SETTLEMENT OF GRACEFUL STONE HOUSES BOASTS A WORKING WOOLEN MILL, FOUNDED IN 1772. BUS LEAVES AT 9 A.M., RETURNS 3 P.M. BOX LUNCHES PROVIDED. The home organized six or eight of these trips during the course of a year, but Arthur could never get his grandfather to go. "I'm not a school kid," Sam would say. "These trips are for school kids."

Arthur stepped back from the bulletin board just as a group of senior citizens was being led toward the exit by relatives. The old people were bundled up in heavy clothes, overdressed actually, for it wasn't that cold. There was, Arthur thought, something to what his grandfather said. There was a tendency to treat old people like children, to patronize them and overprotect, to assume they would be satisfied with less and tolerate more abuse. Arthur headed for the elevators. He wondered if someday he himself would not wind up in a place like this. After all, he was alone, no one to look after him. Perhaps, one mild autumn morning, he might find himself tightly gripping a metal walker, dressed in a warm sweater, winter coat, and heavy woolen hat, shuffling toward the door of a bus that would take him to Dickeyville.

When Arthur entered Sam's room he found Arnie, his grandfather's roommate, seated stiffly on the bed. Arnie was a tiny white-haired man with a ruddy complexion, neat mustache, and twinkling, elfin eyes. Dressed in his blue cab-driver cap, gray muffler, mittens, earmuffs, and buckle boots, only his face distinguished him from an eight-year-old child.

"Arnie," said Arthur, "you look like you're ready to build a snowman."

"I could," said Arnie. "You think I couldn't?"

"I wouldn't put anything past you, Arnie."

"You *couldn't* put anything past me. There's only one thing stopping me right now from running out and building a snowman. No snow."

"Soon," said Arthur, "you'll have your chance." He looked at Sam, seated on the other bed. The room was about ten feet by thirteen; two beds, a shared night table, a wardrobe, and a small dresser constituted the furniture. "So," said Arthur, "you ready to go, Sam?"

Sam nodded. "What are my choices?"

"You don't have to. No one's forcing you."

"I'll go, I'll go."

Sam, Arthur knew, liked to be persuaded. He opened the closet and removed Sam's coat.

"I hope the turkey isn't dry," said Arnie.

"Why should it be dry?" said Sam.

"Why? Because that's how most people cook a turkey. They don't know what the hell they're doing. They cook it the night before, freeze it, then heat it up the next day so it comes out dry. Sticks in your throat." Arnie pointed to his neck.

"I don't know where you get your information," said Sam. "How the hell do you know how most people cook turkeys. What did you do, take a survey?"

"I know," said Arnie. "Believe me, take my word."

"Well, today's turkey will be terrific," said Sam. "My grandson makes friends only with people who cook the same day, fresh."

Arnie turned to Arthur. "You sure this Warren fellow doesn't mind me coming along?"

"No, it's fine," said Arthur. "Absolutely. It's just a big open house, millions of people. You'll see, you'll enjoy it."

"Sounds like the Salvation Army," said Arnie.

Arthur held up his grandfather's coat. "Put your arm in here, Sam."

Sam rose slowly and carefully placed his arms in the sleeves. Arnie turned to face him. "You got your teeth? Where are your teeth?"

Sam probed gingerly at his vacant mouth.

"You gotta have teeth if you're gonna eat turkey," said Arnie, chuckling.

Sam looked around uncertainly.

"Where are your teeth, Grandpa?" said Arthur.

"Did I have teeth the last time you were here?"

"Of course you had teeth," said Arnie.

"When did you last see them?" asked Arthur.

"He had teeth this morning," offered Arnie. He shook his head. "He doesn't remember so good."

"You better watch what you're saying," said Sam. He pointed to Arthur. "My grandson could punch you in the mouth."

Arnie shook with laughter. "My grandson is bigger than your grandson—only he's in California."

"I wish I knew what I did with those teeth," said Sam.

Sam opened the night table drawer and checked inside. He surveyed the tops of the beds and peered at the dresser. Meanwhile, Arnie had climbed off the mattress and sidled up to Arthur. "He's very proud of you, you know."

"I'm proud of him," said Arthur.

"Always talks about his grandson who's going to be a lawyer."

"I wish he could remember that I *am* a lawyer."

Arnie shrugged, not an easy gesture in his bundled condition. "Sometimes he does, sometimes he doesn't. What's the difference? He's still proud of you."

"Arnie!" called Sam from near the window. "You sure I had teeth this morning?"

"You had, you had. Maybe they fell out the window." Arnie turned back to Arthur. "He opens the window a hundred times a day."

"I have to," said Sam. "You keep closing it."

"I know you had them," said Arnie. He looked around. "Wait a minute, what's that . . . on the clock?"

Sam walked over to the clock on the dresser, picked up his teeth, and put them in his mouth

"All right," said Sam. "I'm ready." He started toward the door.

Arthur picked up Sam's hat and gloves. "Don't forget these," he called.

Sam waived disdainfully from the hall.

"Come on, Arnie," said Arthur.

Arnie moved across the room. "I hope they don't have yams," he said in the hall, as Arthur closed the door behind him. "I hate yams."

9

THE house was a large, yellow, asbestos-shingled Colonial with a huge circular driveway and clumps of white birch trees on an otherwise bare expanse of lawn. The sounds of rock music and the chatter of two dozen lawyers and their families were audible from a hundred yards away. Arthur parked on the street and led Sam and Arnie to the pillared front entrance.

"I have a stomachache," said Arnie. "Maybe I should go back."

"Come on," said Arthur, "we're here already. Relax."

Inside, Fresnell's wife greeted them and took their coats. "Warren's mingling somewhere," she said, leading them toward a buffet table filled with platters of sliced turkey, scarlet discs of cranberry, steaming roast beef, noodle pudding, corn, and a host of fragrant potato concoctions. "Help yourself," she added. "Bar's in the corner."

Arthur thanked her and turned back to Arnie and Sam. "You guys find seats, I'll get the drinks. What're you having?"

"Nothing for me," said Arnie.

"I'll get my own," said Sam.

Arthur pushed through the crowd toward the bar. He spotted Fresnell by the blender, stuffing bananas into it. Next to him were an attractive woman in her twenties and an older-looking man. "Have you had one of my daiquiris?" Fresnell was saying. "I don't think you've had one."

"Yes. Yes, I have," said the woman.

Fresnell added some rum. "You know, with my daiquiris, two is the limit."

"Why's that?" asked the woman.

"More than two, you throw up," said Arthur, smiling and extending his hand toward Fresnell.

Fresnell shook it. "More than two, you lose your virginity," he said. He pressed the button on the blender, watched as the drink was beaten to foamy whiteness, and poured it into four glasses on the bar. He handed one glass to the woman and one to the older man. "Just keep your eye on her, Bob. After this she'll do whatever you want."

The man smiled thinly and led the woman away. Fresnell handed one of the remaining daiquiris to Arthur, then drained half the fourth glass himself. "Old cocker," he said, wiping his lips. "Chasing after young women. Wouldn't know what to do with her . . . Gimme one night with her, she'll be calling me at the office, begging . . ."

"Sweet dreams," said Arthur, sipping the drink. "Happy Thanksgiving."

On the staircase, Sam and Arnie sat side by side, each with a paper plate and plastic fork.

"I don't like eating off my knees," said Sam.

"Better than *on* your knees," said Arnie.

"What happened to sitting at a table? You say, 'Pass the salt, A little more stuffing if you don't mind.' That's the type of thing I like."

"You want formal, go to a wedding," said Arnie. "How can they have formal here, they got five thousand people all coming at different times."

Sam wrinkled his nose. "Even so, somehow, eating buffet, with your plate out and standing in line, I always feel like it's the Salvation Army. And the plastic forks, they break as soon as you—" He stopped when he saw Arnie staring intently into his food, not listening.

"You can tell this is catered," said Arnie. "You know how you can tell?"

"How?"

"I don't know. But you can tell. The turkey. And look at this fancy thing here. No one makes this at home." He pointed gingerly at something covered with colored miniature marshmallows.

"You don't like it, don't eat it," said Sam.

"I bet it's yams," said Arnie.

"So give it to me."

"They're trying to hide the yams so I'll eat 'em. Shame on them. To fool an old man."

At the bar, Fresnell was working on another batch of daiquiris. "You hear about the prison boat?" he asked Arthur.

"Nothing," said Arthur.

A tall man next to him swiveled around. "Inner Harbor didn't want it," he said.

"They didn't?" said Fresnell. "Then where'd it go?"

"Last I heard," said the tall man, "they took it to Sparrow's Point, but they didn't want it either, so it's on the move again. I think I'll donate my pool and—" A woman next to him tapped him forcefully on the back and he turned to look. "Oh, my God . . . ," he said slowly.

The room suddenly seemed to grow quieter. People who had been laughing and talking were abruptly whispering. Arthur stood on tiptoe and strained to see over the crowd. A moving pocket had formed in the living room as a man and his wife swept through. The man was bald as an egg.

"Who is it?" asked Fresnell, shutting off the blender.

Arthur came down off his toes. "It's Jay," he said softly. He watched as the Porters slowly made their way toward him. The conversations began to resume as Jay passed and greeted several people. Jay was smiling broadly when he finally drew alongside the bar.

"Well now," said Fresnell, turning toward Arthur, "what do you think?"

Arthur looked at Jay's wife. "If Sally likes him bald, it's fine with me."

Sally glanced back at Arthur for the briefest instant, time enough nevertheless to transmit her intense distress.

Arthur put his hand on Jay's shoulder. "Gotta talk to you for a minute."

Jay waved to the small group of people who had gathered around. "Later, each and every one of you will be allowed to pet it."

Arthur could hear the chuckling behind him as he led Jay to an unoccupied corner near one of the hallways. "You okay?" he asked.

"Sure," said Jay. "No problem."

"Why the bald head?"

"A lark."

"Just a lark?"

"Yeah."

"You got up and shaved your head for a lark?"

"Yeah."

Arthur considered. It was possible. . . . He himself had once, several years ago, grown a full beard, then shaved it off after a month. People bought peculiar hats on impulse, shoes. It was possible.

"I see you're searching for other motives," said Jay. "No, no—"

"Also, it strengthens the hair—supposed to make it grow back thicker. In case you hadn't noticed, mine was tending toward the wispy side."

"Look, you don't owe me any explanations," said Arthur.

"Thank you," said Jay. "Glad to hear you acknowledge that."

"I just—you sure nothing's bothering you?"

"Arthur," said Jay, tired, "stop playing big brother." He strode rapidly away.

Arthur finished his daiquiri. A voice behind him

said, "It's true that Fleming passed the polygraph test, isn't it?" Arthur looked around. It was Larry Corning, a porcine, ultracautious real-estate lawyer, best known for his insistence that even the most trivial request of him be put in writing and signed—"His wife has to fill out forms in triplicate before he'll do it," other lawyers would comment about him.

"Larry," said Arthur now, "anything relating to Fleming is privileged information."

Corning was slightly drunk. "Yeah, well let's just say I'm one of the privileged."

"Sorry," said Arthur.

"He did, didn't he?" persisted Corning.

Arthur began to move away, but Corning followed.

"What are the odds on that?" asked Corning. "Nobody wants to believe he's innocent."

Arthur walked faster. "I really don't want to talk about it."

Corning stopped. "Yeah, well . . . if you win the case you'll have to put a take-a-number machine in your office."

An hour later, eight of the men had gone outside to the concrete patio and were taking desultory shots at a basketball hoop mounted on a metal pole. Since everyone had been drinking, few of the shots went in.

"I see two rims," said one of the lawyers.

"All the easier to score," said Fresnell. He grabbed a rebound and held the ball. "Okay. Enough warmups. The Fifth Annual Thanksgiving Toilet Bowl is about to begin."

Four of the men demurred, leaving Arthur, Jay, Fresnell, and Corning as the only players.

"Two same fingers are together," said Fresnell.

"Oh, bullshit," Arthur said. "Jay and I against you and Larry. Whaddaya say?"

Fresnell glanced at Corning. "Fine," said Fresnell. "Since we're playing on a new court this year, courtesy of a beautiful home purchased on the money from the misfortunate, the injured, and the criminal community, bless their hearts, I—"

"He's so bombed," Arthur said to Jay, "I bet he can't remember the beginning of his sentence."

"—will now explain the boundary lines. Edge of the grass is out, the house is out, you put the ball in bounds near the window. After a basket, the opposite—"

"Come on, come on," said Jay. "Street rules. We all know how to play. Let's go."

"You take it out," said Fresnell.

Jay stood on the edge of the grass and whipped a pass in for Arthur. Arthur dribbled slowly with his right hand until he saw Fresnell come up, then suddenly crossed the ball in front of him to his left. Fresnell's daiquiri-dulled reflexes were too slow to make the steal; before he realized what was happening Arthur was by him and in for an easy left-handed lay-up.

Jay screamed and thrust both hands in the air. "We score!" he yelled. "Waaaaoooooooeeeee! We score! We score! Woo, woo, woo!"

Fresnell took the ball out of bounds.

"Hey, same team!" yelled Jay. "Team that scored gets the ball. Street rules."

"No, no," said Fresnell. "These are house rules. It's my ball." He grinned.

Jay stamped his foot.

"It doesn't matter," said Arthur. "Let him have it."

Fresnell threw a looping pass for Corning, who faked left, then right, then left again. He dribbled inside and was just about to go up for the shot when Jay smashed into him, knocking him over.

Corning rose slowly from the concrete. "Foul! Hey, I got fouled!"

"Bullshit!" said Jay heatedly. "You were charging. No foul. Let's play." He grabbed the ball and threw it to Arthur. "Put it in play."

Arthur looked over at Corning who stood rubbing an elbow. "You okay?"

"Yeah," Corning said grumpily.

"Can I have a written release?" said Arthur.

"All right, wise guy," said Corning, "let's play the game."

Arthur threw a bounce pass to Jay, who dribbled in toward the basket, took it back outside, then dribbled around near the edges of the court, and was beginning once more to move in when Corning reached around and stole the ball. He coasted to the basket for an easy two points. Jay pounded his fist again and again into his palm.

Inside, Sam, Arnie, and a retired lawyer named Jake Zeller watched the action through a window.

"Look at them," said Sam. "The game makes no sense."

"It's a game," said Arnie.

"They run and run. For what?"

"To run."

"You would think that a group of professional people wouldn't take such a game so seriously. Look how serious they are, especially the bald one." Sam shook his head.

"That's your grandson's partner," said Zeller.

"They're all lawyers out there?"

Zeller nodded. "And in here. All lawyers. They say, nationwide, we have one lawyer for every five hundred people. And that the ratio diminishes each year."

"They produce them like yams," said Arnie.

"Someone wrote," said Zeller, "that by our Tricentennial we'll be fortunate if any Americans but lawyers are alive to see it."

Outside, the sun was beginning to set. Despite the encroaching cold, the men's faces were drenched with perspiration. Fresnell was wheezing. Corning had wrapped his tie around his forehead and was using it as a sweatband. Arthur's shirt was open, and his sleeves rolled up. His tie had long ago been consigned to a rear pocket. Only Jay seemed relatively unaffected by the constant effort; he stood hands on hips, red-faced, but otherwise showing no sign of fatigue.

"Your ball," said Arthur, dead tired but not wanting to be the first to quit. "Eighteen—fourteen."

Fresnell tossed it to Corning, then cut for the basket, caught a crisp return pass, and went in for the score. Arthur took the ball out of bounds. He threw it in to Jay, who began dribbling erratically. Suddenly, he stopped and tried to force a pass to Arthur, but Corning, anticipating, easily stole the ball away. He was dribbling in toward the basket when Jay again barreled into him. Corning sank to the concrete.

"Foul!" yelled Fresnell. "Foul, again!"

"No way!" screamed Jay. "No way!"

"You fouled, Jay," said Arthur, watching his partner carefully.

"He charged me!"

Corning slowly rose to his feet. "You're crazy, you know that. There's something wr—"

Jay punched him in the face. For a moment both men stood paralyzed, Jay watching the effect, Corning frozen with the stunning pain. When he finally grabbed his cheek and began to reel backward, Jay went at him again, swinging wild roundhouse lefts and rights. Fresnell, next to Jay, tried to grab him around the waist, but Jay twisted in his arms and redirected his attack at Fresnell. Arthur attempted to pull the two men apart as Corning staggered near the edge of the patio and several men ran out of the house to try and help. Somehow, Jay was able to hold them all off, kicking one in the leg, biting another on the hand, choking a third with his own tie. It seemed that no one could stop him until Arthur, in the confusion, finally landed a sneak punch to Jay's stomach that set him doubling over and gasping for air.

"All right, give him room!" ordered Arthur. "Give him room!"

The crowd of men slowly backed off. Jay was down on one knee, coughing and gagging.

"It's over," Arthur said to him. "All right?" He fought to catch his own breath. "It's over."

Arthur and Ralph Agee took the courthouse elevator up to the third floor. Arthur had emphasized previously the importance of Agee's attire; anything that removed him further from the normal heterosexual world might act to dehumanize him before the court. Judges were human beings; they had conscious and subconscious prejudices. In a borderline case, a blatant transvestite might be found guilty when someone else could be declared innocent. If found guilty, the transvestite's sentence might be harsher. The idea was to appear, as closely as possible, to be a member of the judge's own social and economic class. Make him see a part of himself standing before that bench.

Agee had done as well as he could. He wore a blue shirt and black trousers, both of which hung loosely on his skinny frame. On his head, however, the blond wig was still perched demurely, although it was pulled back into a neat little bun.

"Ralph," said Arthur, as the elevator doors opened. "Do you think, maybe, you could take off the wig?"

"What for?" said Agee.

"Ralph, I explained all that."

Agee shuddered. "I can't," he said. "I feel naked enough just as I am." They walked through the corridor, Agee's eyes bulging nearly out of his head, muscles writhing under his cheeks. "Do I have to?" he asked, as they neared Courtroom A.

Arthur put his arm on Agee's shoulder. "Take it easy," he said. And then, softly, "No, you don't have to."

An hour later they were seated at the defense table, Judge Burns staring down at them from the bench. The judge nodded to the bailiff.

"Will the defendant please rise."

Agee and Arthur stood up. Agee was shaking uncontrollably.

"I find the defendant, Ralph Agee, guilty of armed robbery," said Burns. He banged the gavel.

Agee turned to Arthur. "What's goin' on?"

"He found you guilty," said Arthur.

"I don't understand. Am I goin' to jail?" His face contorted in horror as his voice rose. "I can't go to jail."

Arthur addressed the judge, his voice calm and steady. "Your Honor, in light of the fact that this is the defendant's first major offense, that he is currently employed, and otherwise has a good record, I request a presentence investigation."

"You foresee a favorable probation report?" asked the judge.

"Yes, Your Honor, I do." Agee worked as a sweeper and go-fer in a barber shop. That the barber was also a small-time bookie and that Agee often carried betting slips would not show up on the report.

Judge Burns gathered a group of papers in front of him. "Make note," he told the court clerk. "A probation report is to be drawn up and presented to this court within fifteen days. Sentencing will be withheld until that time." He lightly tapped the gavel. "Court is adjourned until two o'clock."

Arthur began collecting the Manila folders on the defense table and stuffing them into his briefcase.

"What happens now?" asked Agee. A guard stood waiting several feet away.

"They draw up the report and present it to the judge," said Arthur.

"But now—"

Arthur thought Agee might begin to cry. "For now, you have to wait."

"Oh, man," Agee moaned.

An elderly black woman made her way toward them through the spectators' section.

"Have courage," said Arthur. "In fifteen days you should get off on probation."

"Should?" said Agee, his voice high-pitched, nearly a shriek. "I gotta be! Oh, man, I got to."

"Don't worry," said Arthur. "Take it easy. You'll be okay, you'll be okay."

The black woman was through the gate and cradling Agee in her arms as Arthur and the guard looked on. Agee's face was buried in her gray hair. "Momma," he kept repeating. "Oh, Momma. I can't go to jail."

Sherry handed the photographs to Arthur one by one. They were police pictures of Leah Shepard, and they concentrated on her upper torso and face. A back view showed deep cuts and bruises starting from her shoulders and extending nearly to her waist. There were angry welts on her breasts. Her cheeks were black and blue, and both eyes were swollen nearly shut. Arthur inhaled deeply and replaced the photos in the envelope. He studied the statement of Leah Shepard's report. Fleming had asked her out on a date. They had gone to dinner and then seen a movie. He took her back to her house and she invited him in. They danced for a while and had a few drinks. Fleming then "started to get aggressive" and she asked him to leave, which he did. Ten minutes later, she heard a knock on the door. It was Fleming, claiming he had forgotten his gloves. When she opened the door, he punched her in the neck, forced his way in, and started to choke her. He beat her about the head and shoulders and began ripping off her clothes. He threatened to kill her if she resisted. Then, after tying her to the bed and stuffing a handkerchief in her mouth, he raped her. She passed out. When she regained consciousness, he was gone.

Arthur gazed at some additional documents, then looked up. "Baltimore County Hospital records show that Leah Shepard had a D and C in nineteen sixty-eight," he said to Sherry. "She was eighteen at the time. I don't know if a D and C is a normal procedure at that age. Call Doctor Edwards and check that out."

"What's this?" Arthur asked as he handed Sherry a scrap of paper that was mixed in with the police documents.

"Oh. That's the name and address of the guy who lives near Leah Shepard's house. He may be a possible witness."

"I guess I'd better go and see him myself," Arthur sighed as he crammed Reisler's address into his jacket pocket.

As Arthur pulled up in front of Reisler's house he saw a man, he presumed Reisler, walking a huge, black and gray bull mastiff. Arthur was feeling a little uneasy about the powerfully built dog and so called out, "Mr. Reisler?" from the safe confines of his car.

"I think he's constipated," Reisler said matter-of-factly as he motioned to the dog, who was now sniffing at a tree, looking generally disinterested.

"I'm Art Kirkland," said Arthur as he began to ease out of the car. "I called before."

"How do." Reisler noticed Arthur's trepidation and tried to reassure him. "Nothing to be afraid of. Old Ronald, here, is really a pussycat."

"Uh, sure. No problem," murmured Arthur. He wanted so much to believe him. "Mr. Reisler . . ." started Arthur.

"Bob, please. The only person that calls me Mr. Reisler is my mother-in-law."

Arthur smiled. He knew that he would have to humor this witness a bit. He was not a man to be pushed. Reisler was of medium build, in his mid-fifties. There was an air about him that told Arthur he would have to coddle him to get the information that he wanted. "Okay, Bob it is."

"Uh, Bob, why don't you tell me about the man you told the police you saw going into Leah Shepard's house," Arthur asked congenially.

"Didn't tell the police," Reisler said.

"What?" Arthur was getting upset. He would have

to control that. "Uh, what do you mean, Mr. Re—er, Bob?"

"Spent four hours in that police station waiting for somebody to take my statement. That's what you call it, right? A statement?" Reisler was obviously enjoying his role as a key witness.

"Yes. That's right. A statement," said Arthur.

"Well, anyway . . . nobody paid any attention, so I left."

"Jesus!" Arthur snapped. His annoyance was momentarily transferred. "Why don't you tell me what you saw then, Bob. *I'm* listening."

"I happened to notice that article in the paper, you know, the one about Judge Fleming . . ."

"Yes?" Arthur said anxiously.

"Well, they mentioned that the judge said somebody must have come in after he'd left the girl's house."

"So?"

"Finally it occurred to me that the address of the Shepard girl's house is around the corner from me. Dorset. I live on Oswego. It's not a bad neighborhood actu—"

"Mr. Reisler . . . I mean, Bob," interrupted Arthur, "is all this leading somewhere?"

"Oh, yes," said Reisler. "Definitely. See, after I read the article, I went to take a look at the house—you know, curiosity and all." Reisler laughed then, a kind of snort-on-the-inhale that Arthur at first thought came from the dog. "Anyway," continued Reisler, "I realized that was the house I always look at when I walk Ronald down the block."

"Why is that?" asked Arthur.

"Cause it's the only one on the street that isn't painted. It's natural brick, you know, very attractive. I've been thinking of sandblasting mine, but the missus doesn't really . . ."

"And?" said Arthur, no longer able to conceal his impatience.

"I saw somebody go into her house that night . . . you know, when that thing happened."

Arthur became alert. "What time was that?"

"I walk Ronald right after Johnny Carson."

"You always walk down that street?"

"No. Sometimes I go down Granada, sometimes Eldorado," replied Reisler.

"Then how can you be sure that on that particular night you . . ."

"It's a routine," interrupted Reisler. "I alternate every third night. That way people don't always complain about dog poop on their lawn." He reached down and scratched Ronald's neck.

"Are you sure you were on Dorset that night?"

"Oh, yeah. Like I said, it's a set routine. We're on Dorset every Wednesday and Saturday."

Arthur's brow furrowed. He was finding this conversation extremely difficult. "Wednesday and . . . no good. It doesn't work."

"What?"

"Three streets in seven days. You wouldn't be on the same street every Wednesday."

Reisler held up his thumb. "Sure it does. Here. Granada on Monday, right?" An index finger popped out as Arthur nodded. "Eldorado on Tuesday." Middle finger. "Dorset on Wednesday." Ring finger. "Granada on Thursday." Pinky. "Eldorado, Friday." Thumb of second hand. "Dorset, Saturday . . . and Sunday I spend with my sister in Velvet Valley."

"Ah, yes," Arthur said as he nodded his understanding.

"My dog takes his poop out there," said Reisler. He reached down and stroked the dog's ear. "Poor Ronald," he said. "He's been breaking out in rashes. Can't stop scratching himself. You know what the vet said it was?"

Arthur had an urge to say, "Syph," but restrained himself.

"Acne," said Reisler. "I've got to take him off fatty foods."

Arthur nodded in feigned sympathy. "Mr. Reisler, what did this man look like?"

The sixty-four-dollar question.

"Tall," said Reisler. "I'd guess six-foot-four, at least. Minimum, six-two. And blond hair."

"You're sure?" Fleming was about five-nine, with black hair.

"Yes."

"Mr. Reisler, I notice you're not wearing glasses now. Do you use them at any time?"

"Nope. Don't need to. Always had perfect vision. Everyone in my family does."

"Wasn't it dark out at that time?"

"Certainly was."

"Then how could you see?"

"Street lamp," said Reisler. " 'Bout, oh, twenty feet away, I'd say."

Arthur stood up. "Mr. Reisler, are you certain of everything you've told me?" Arthur could hardly believe his luck. The man was a solid citizen, an engineer yet, a trained observer, difficult to shake up on a witness stand—it was incredible!

"Of course I'm certain," said Reisler.

"Would you be willing to testify in court about what you told me?" asked Arthur. He came around in front of the tree.

"Yes, well . . ." said Reisler. "I guess, if I have to."

Arthur knelt and scratched Ronald under the ears. "You're a nice dog," he said. "And don't worry. I'll get you some Clearasil."

10

HE was descending the courthouse steps when he heard a horn honking insistently. A Cadillac pulled up to the curb and Carl Bennett leaned out the front window. "Hey, Arthur? Arthur, over here!"

Arthur walked toward him, forcing a smile.

"Where you headed?" asked Bennett.

"Office."

"Get in. I'll take you."

Arthur was beginning to formulate an excuse for not going when he remembered something he had thought of that morning. He walked around, and got in next to Bennett.

"Arthur," said Bennett, "I got a problem with this young girl." They pulled away.

"Again?"

"Well, you know me."

Bennett detailed his difficulties as they rode. It was an old story. For an intelligent executive, he was always managing to pick the most vicious and greedy women to have illicit affairs with. "What can I do?" he moaned. "I'm a basically shallow person. I go only by looks. Can I help it if the beautiful ones are also the nastiest?"

"Not all beautiful women, Carl," said Arthur. "Can't you ever find one who lets you off the hook gracefully?"

"I don't know," said Bennett. "They all seem to

end up either blackmailing me or suing me, or both. But I swear, this time I'm not the father."

"May I make a suggestion?" said Arthur.

"Anything."

"Cut your balls off. It gives you a margin of error."

They stopped in a small shacklike restaurant on a wharf in Baltimore Harbor, its rotten wooden furnishings suggesting a kind of piscine elegance. They sat by a window and ordered steamed crabs for two. Bennett glanced out the window and kept staring as something caught his eye. "Isn't that the prison ship?"

Arthur looked out also. "Uh huh."

"Where's it going?"

"Well, so far I've heard it's been turned down by four harbor communities."

"So where's it headed now?"

"They're taking it down to Annapolis."

"They have an acceptance?"

"Who knows?" said Arthur. "If they can't stay there, they may take it inland."

"There's no body of water inland," said Carl.

Arthur looked away from the window. "That's right."

Arthur sat up impatiently against the headboard, while Gail stood in the bathroom doorway wearing only a pair of thin panties and leisurely brushing her hair. Was it possible that she was unaware of how appealing she looked? She seemed to be in no rush.

"So is Jay letting his hair grow back, or keeping it shaved?"

"Shaves it every day," said Arthur, trying to keep his voice casual. "He carries a battery-operated razor. just keeps running it over the top of his head all day long."

Gail's nipples stood out as her upraised arms formed a graceful curve. "That sounds pretty bad."

Arthur shrugged. "Well, most men shave their faces every day. Jay just goes a little higher, that's all. It's been done before.

"It's been done before," Gail agreed, "but in Jay's case it's not normal." She stopped the brushing and faced him. "Is it?"

Arthur simply could not tear his eyes away from her. Somehow, with an item of clothing still on, she was even more sensual, more alluring than when completely naked. "Jay will be fine," he said. "Just fine." He tapped the bed beside him. "How about keeping me company?"

Gail narrowed her eyes. "What have you got in mind?"

"Come and find out."

She put the hairbrush back in the medicine cabinet and walked over to the bed. She sat down next to Arthur, and he put his hand on her shoulder, inhaling the fragrance of her skin. "You know," she said, "the committee's considering calling him in."

Arthur removed his hand.

"Well, I mean, he did shave his head."

"I wasn't aware that was a violation of legal ethics. Is the committee going after bald lawyers now?"

"He continually postpones his court cases. . . ."

"Look," said Arthur, "Jay just needs a little time."

"You think that will bring him out of it?"

"I think so, yes. I've taken over most of his trial work. He has only a few more court cases left and then he's through. He's putting his emphasis on contracts. So lay off, okay?"

Gail moved to the foot of the bed. "It's not up to me," she said.

"I tell you, it's really ironic." Arthur looked up at the ceiling. "Every day hundreds of defense lawyers are busy getting clients off. Guilty or innocent, it doesn't make any difference."

"No one ever claimed the system is perfect," said Gail. "Where's my bra?"

"And the guilty ones are right back out there, robbing, killing, raping, beating—you name it. The lawyer's job ends in the courtroom. Whatever happens after that doesn't affect him."

"Arthur, everyone understands that lawyers are human beings. And they're not unique either. What about engineers who design missiles? Doctors who heal homicidal lunatics? People need a certain detachment, a certain insularity. No moral code requires assuming responsibility for every possible consequence of your actions. Where's my bra?"

"Then you're saying a lawyer is wrong to let such things affect him. His only concern should be protecting the rights of his client."

"I'm saying it's a matter of degree . . . like everything else in life." She straightened her back. "Please, Arthur—my bra. I'd like to know where it is."

Arthur was rapidly losing interest in lovemaking. "Forget that," he said. "The only difference between Jay and all those thousands of other lawyers is that he was *affected . . . hurt . . . injured.*"

"I understand that, but—"

"And so the irony is that the one lawyer, the only lawyer, who *felt* something is the one who may be called up before the Ethics Committee."

Gail screwed up her face in frustration, an expression Arthur found exceedingly attractive. "That's not fair, Arthur."

"I think it's perfectly accurate."

"I mean, I know Jay is hurting. The point is, he's not functioning properly because of it."

"Well then, help him, don't hurt him."

"Arthur, no one will hurt him."

"It will hurt him if he's called before that committee. It's persecuting him."

"Arthur, I won't discuss this further until I get my bra. I can't argue persuasively while I'm half-naked."

"Forget that," said Arthur. "If you want my opinion, that enhances your arguing ability. But we'll

129

overlook that now. The fact is, you go after Jay, or whoever, but you won't touch Judge Rayford, who is a suicidal maniac. Don't get me wrong. I love the guy and I don't want you to touch him . . . but he is bent on killing himself."

"What do you mean?"

"Every Sunday he flies a helicopter and tries not to return alive."

"Who told you that?"

"I went up with him once. I came down twenty years older. They had to jump-start my heart."

"It sounds incredible."

"It's no secret," said Arthur, "that a court bailiff found him in his chambers trying to hang himself. He'd have made it too, but the light fixture he looped the rope around was so old it just pulled out of the ceiling."

"People know about this?"

"Sure. Everyone who spends time in the courthouse knows. And another thing—where do you think Rayford has lunch every day?"

"I gather it's not McDonald's."

"Sitting outside his window, on the ledge, four stories up. Rain or shine, sleet or hail, the judge completes his faithfully appointed rounds fifty feet above the sidewalk."

"He's sick," said Gail dazedly.

"Probably," said Arthur. "But at least he's a human being. Some thing or some one or some condition has moved him so deeply that he wants to obliterate himself." He held up a hand. "But, I agree, this is abnormal behavior. Imagine a man in that frame of mind making decisions about people's lives every day."

"He's an excellent judge," said Gail softly.

"And Jay's an excellent lawyer."

Gail hesitated. "I know that, but the committee still wants to see him."

Arthur stared at her, his excitement returning. "You know, there are times when I'm not sure I like you."

130

"Same here."

"I mean, we're so opposite in the way we feel about things."

"That's what makes a horse race," said Gail. She moved a bit upward on the bed.

"But I figure maybe that's good for the relationship," said Arthur.

"Why? Because it keeps us from getting too close?"

"Yeah," said Arthur. He ran his hands up the smoothness of her thighs. "Obviously, neither of us could handle a marriage and a career at the same time."

"Well," said Gail, smiling pertly and creeping slowly toward him, "then it's perfect, as long as we keep a little friction between us." She was on her knees now, straddling him, her breasts dangling over his face.

Arthur reached up "Friction is no problem," he said.

Frank Bowers, an assistant DA, was in a good mood. After his breakfast of diet pineapple chunks on cottage cheese and coffee with skim milk, he had weighed himself on his bathroom scale and found that he had lost three pounds in the last week. *Twelve pounds in five weeks!* he exulted. He could hardly believe it. And then had come his wife's announcement: she would go in for reconstructive surgery on her collapsed vaginal wall. Bowers was ecstatic. No question now—this was his day. So it scarcely came as a surprise, when he called his New York broker, that his stock, Lucky Seven Mines, had opened a dollar a share higher than last night's close. It appeared that only two of the five shafts were flooded. And so Bowers hung up the phone smiling. When you're hot, you're hot, he thought. And on such vagaries depended half a dozen criminal-case defendants.

Bowers stood in the hall of the district court building and slouched against a wall as Leo Fauci, a har-

ried, skinny, scraggly bearded public defender badgered him about various deals. Normally, Bowers would
have been quite irritable and made some excuse to
get away, but today he just stood there, a beatific
expression on his face.

"So," said Fauci, "what can you do?"

Bower's mind wandered. "You notice how bare
everything looked today?"

"What?"

"Driving in. I mean, the leaves are off the trees now
and everything seems, I dunno, so desolate. . . . It's
beautiful, in a way."

Fauci eyed him strangely. He kept referring inter-
mittently to his notepad, as if somewhere, on one of
the pages, might be a clue to what Bowers was talking
about.

"You have a house?" asked Bowers. It was amazing, he thought, how little we know about people we
see every day.

"No," said Fauci, quickly. "No house. Apartment.
Two rooms. Listen, Frank . . ."

Bowers shrugged. "A year," he said arbitrarily.

"What, are you kidding me?"

"Why—a year is bad? The guy had enough hash
to throw a block party."

"I thought this was bargain day," said Fauci.

Bowers nodded. "You're right. Tell me what you
want. No reasonable offer refused."

"Make it six months," said Fauci, "and I think he'll
buy."

"Okay," said Bowers casually. "What else you got?"

Fauci's beard disappeared into the notepad. "Fenwick," he said finally.

Fenwick was a gnarled and twisted degenerate who
somehow had married a beautiful woman. His wife
had finally brought him to court on charges of having
continually raped their two teen-age daughters. At the
arraignment, Bowers had asked him why he did it,
and Fenwick, looking up with hate-filled piercing

132

eyes, had snarled, "Because they were good pieces of ass." Bowers looked now at Fauci. "Eighteen months," he said.

"Eighteen months! Good luck."

"Best I can do."

"Oh," said Fauci. "Well then *you* tell him. That cocksucker's crazy. He'd just as soon snap your neck."

Down the corridor, Bowers spotted Arthur emerging from an elevator. "Well," said Bowers, "I really can't . . . ah, tell you what, make it a year. But the offer's good only for today."

"Frank," whined Fauci, "come on . . ."

Arthur was several yards away.

"Hey," said Bowers. "That's it. Just because I'm in a good mood, don't take advantage."

"I gotta talk to you," Arthur called.

"Here I am," said Bowers. "In the flesh." He motioned to Fauci. "Is that it?"

Fauci stared at his notepad. "Yeah, that's it," he said glumly. "I'll have to get back to you on Fenwick."

"Fine," said Bowers.

Fauci walked off.

"It was a good day until I started with him," said Bowers. "The man is a human barbiturate."

"I have to talk to you," Arthur repeated.

Bowers motioned toward a courtroom. "Come on, I got a case coming up."

The two of them stood just inside the door and watched for a moment as an elderly man testified from the witness stand. ". . . and this punk kept pulling at her purse, and she wouldn't let go. So I tried to get him off, he pushed me away, and then he knocks my wife into a wall, starts banging her head, then grabs the purse, and runs off." The man looked pleadingly up at the judge. "We just came from the bank. Everything was in that bag. Our Social Security . . ."

Arthur and Bowers stood just inside the back door of the courtroom.

"If it was just me," said Bowers, "I'd chuck the whole Fleming thing out the window."

"So do it," said Arthur.

Bowers smiled.

"Come on, Frank, you know I've got you by the balls. Fleming's clean on the polygraph, and I've got an eyewitness."

"Yeah," said Bowers, "I know. But what can I do? If the DA's office drops this case now, everybody will be screaming political deal."

"You're going to come out of this with a lot of egg on your face."

"Maybe. But I have no choice. Now if this was one of your run-of-the-mill Saturday night killings, or something, we could deal. But this is too hot. It's center ring."

On the witness stand, a pockmarked Latin-looking man was speaking directly to the judge. "It wasn't my fault, you know? That old lady, she just kept hanging on. She lets go of that purse an' I'm on my way. But man, she just kept hangin' on, hangin' on. I mean, what am I suppose' to do, hah? Next thing I know—bam!—she slips." He shook his head. "I mean, I don't mean no harm or nothin', you know?"

Bowers turned to Arthur. "I tell you, people are getting real pissed off at the law these days, and I can't really say I blame them." He grinned shrewdly. "Now if I can turn that to my advantage, you may find yourself representing a sacrificial lamb."

"Since we're on the farm now," said Arthur, "my advice is, don't count your chickens."

"Just looking for my seventy-fourth straight win," said Bowers. "Not that I want to be a pig about it, of course."

At the front of the room, Judge Howe, a middle-aged woman, stared appraisingly at the defendant. "All right, Mr. Avilla. I'm going to give you one year probation." She tapped her gavel.

The old man who had testified earlier stood up.

"One year probation! What kind of punishment is that? I got a wife in the hospital with a broken hip. They say she—"

The bailiff started forward but the judge signaled him to stop.

"—may even lose an eye, and you're going to send this person home? To do it again to someone else?"

Judge Howe once more tapped the gravel. Two guards flanked the Latin man at the defense table.

"What kind of justice is that?" shouted the old man. Tears were streaming down his cheeks. A young woman was trying to lead him away.

"Another customer for Don Corleone," whispered Bowers to Arthur.

"All right," said the judge loudly, "what else do we have here this morning?"

11

ARTHUR walked down the hall, pressed the UP button for the elevator. He was going only one floor and knew he should be walking, and yet. . . . He got on and moved inside the car as the doors closed. This is the way we kill ourselves, he thought. We shave years off our lives in ten-second elevator rides, in the automobile to the corner mailbox, in the living room chair on Sunday afternoons. The door opened, and a shot rang out. This *is* the way we kill ourselves, thought Arthur, quickly ducking from the car and flattening himself against a wall.

A second shot came—only it wasn't a shot. It was, Arthur saw . . . a plate. *Crash!* A white porcelain disc shattered against a NO SMOKING sign ten feet ahead of him. Arthur crept along the wall until he came to a group of people huddled just behind an intersection.

"What's going on?" he asked.

A woman turned, "He's mad."

"Who?"

"A lawyer," said the woman. "Jay Porter."

Carefully, Arthur edged his way forward, peeked around the corner into the perpendicular corridor. There, about halfway down, Jay stood tensely by a tall stack of plates. In the crook of his left arm were a half-dozen more, and in his right hand was one all set to be fired. Arthur stuck his head out.

"Keep away!" yelled Jay. "Keep away! I'm not ready!"

"Jay!" called Arthur. "Jay, it's me, Arthur."

Like the world's finest skeet target, the plate came whistling down the corridor to smash against the far wall. Arthur quickly withdrew around the corner.

"Where the hell did he get the plates?" he asked the woman.

"From the cafeteria, I imagine," she said. "Someone said he's been bringing them up all morning. No one paid any attention."

A man poised, then sprinted across the open hallway. A sailing plate missed his head by inches. From a stairwell near the bank of elevators, a uniformed policeman emerged, gun drawn. Trying to localize the source of trouble, he hesitated in the doorway a moment. Finally, as he walked cautiously forward, the woman next to Arthur called out.

"There," she said, pointing. "Down there."

The policeman edged forward.

"He's not armed," said Arthur. "His only weapons are plates."

The policeman looked around the corner. Immediately a plate sailed into the wall above him; a few of the pieces fell on his cap. He ducked back just as the elevator door opened again. Three policemen and Judge Rayford got out.

"We've got trouble here," said the first officer. "Guy's got a stack of plates he's throwing around. I think we got another Nolan Ryan here."

Arthur came back to meet Rayford. "It's Jay," he said.

"You know this guy?" one of the policemen asked the judge.

"Name is Jay Porter," said Rayford. "He's a lawyer. Happens to be a very nice man."

The policeman looked at Rayford quizzically, then moved to the intersection and put his mouth near the corner. "Mr. Porter," he yelled.

Jay answered with a plate.

"Mr. Porter, how 'bout forgetting the frisbee game?"

"I'm not ready yet!" yelled Jay.

"What's he talking about?" asked the first policeman. "Not ready for what?"

"No one knows," said the woman who stood near Arthur. "That's all he keeps yelling."

Jay rocked nervously back and forth on his heels. He was breathing heavily and perspiring, and every once in a while he seemed to hum slightly or moan, no one could tell which. He looked terrified, pathetic.

"I'm going to try to rush him," said the first policeman. He braced himself against the wall.

Jay cocked his arm.

"Now!" said the policeman, pushing off and racing down the hall.

Jay fired one plate over the cop's head, another a foot in front of him. When a third ricocheted off a wall and he still had ten yards to go, the policeman abruptly turned and retreated.

"He's too fast," he gasped as he rounded the corner. "The man is just too damn quick."

"I told you I wasn't ready!" Jay screamed. "I'm not ready!"

"Screw this," said the second policeman. "Get the canisters. We'll gas him out."

"Wait!" said Arthur. He turned to Rayford. "Christ! We've got to do something!"

Rayford nodded. His body stiffened. "I'll take command. You agree?"

"Right."

"I'll run interference." The judge paused. "Are you with me?"

"What are you going to interfere with?"

Rayford held up his briefcase. "I got this. Ready?"

"Yes."

The second policeman was speaking into a walkie-talkie. "We're going to need some assistance up here, Glenn. A couple of canisters . . . and you better get an ambulance."

"Excuse me, gentlemen," said Rayford as he and Arthur nudged past. "Judge coming through." He turned to Arthur. "All set?"

Arthur nodded.

"Stay right on my tail . . . *now!*"

Rayford bolted from the corner and ran a zigzag blocking pattern down the hall, briefcase out in front, Arthur close behind. Jay responded to the challenge with a barrage of plates, a virtual squadron of circular missiles. Only three of them actually came close, however, and Rayford easily picked those off with his briefcase. Five yards away, he threw the case at Jay, then launched himself through the air, bowling Jay over backward. Arthur grabbed his partner's left arm and Rayford pinned the right, as Jay struggled furiously.

"Don't you understand!" he screamed. "I'm not ready!"

And then somehow, for an instant, he broke away, toppling the entire remaining stack of plates before Arthur and Rayford could pin him down again. From the corner of his eye, Arthur could see the policemen racing down the hall.

138

"I'm not ready, Judge!" Jay screamed. "I'm not ready to try this case. I'm not prepared! Need time to prepare it. I'm not ready!"

Arthur leaned heavily on Jay's arm, stared at his reddened, sweaty face. Jay's eyes were darting frantically back and forth; human restraint and temperance were gone, replaced by the aggressive fear of a cornered-animal. "Oh, God," said Arthur.

Arthur stood with Warren Fresnell on the courthouse steps and watched as two attendants loaded Jay into the back of the ambulance. He was wearing a strait jacket and screaming unintelligibly, leather straps held him to the gurney. A small, curious crowd looked on as the ambulance pulled away. Arthur shuddered; mental breakdowns were, in many ways, far more frightening than physical ailments. The latter, after all, were understandable, if not necessarily curable. Bacteria and viruses invaded tissues and caused disease. Stones blocked kidneys and gall bladders. Plaque deposits occluded coronary arteries. Falls from heights broke bones. But mental illness? The very essence of your being changed mysteriously, done in by an idea, a few words, a subtle alteration in the synaptic chemicals of the brain. The terror, of course, lay in the obscurity of the causes, the pervasiveness of the effects—and the realization that you might be next.

"Arthur. Arthur!"

Arthur looked around slowly.

"Art, you okay?"

It was Fresnell.

"Yeah," said Arthur slowly. "Yeah, I just . . . listen, I gotta go. I'm meeting Jay's wife at the hospital." He reached down into his briefcase and pulled out a folder. "I really appreciate this, Warren."

"No problem," said Fresnell, taking the folder and putting it in his attaché case.

"Ralph Agee," said Arthur. "He'll be wearing a blond wig, but don't let that throw you."

"I've seen blond wigs before," said Fresnell.

"Let him keep it on. It's like a security blanket, makes him happy. They're just going to review his probation report. I checked it, it's screwed up."

"As usual."

"The corrections are in the folder," said Arthur.

Fresnell was looking at a brunette with black mesh stockings and spike heels. "Love them all," he murmured as she climbed the steps.

"Warren," said Arthur, "you'll remember? They're on a yellow sheet in the back. Make sure the judge sees it."

"Right, right," said Fresnell. He turned back to Arthur. "Art, don't worry so much. Go take care of your partner."

"You should be in and out in five minutes," said Arthur.

"I got plenty of time," said Fresnell. "No problem."

"Tell Agee I'm sorry I can't be there myself."

"I'll tell him."

"Tell him I'll call him at home tonight."

Fresnell waved Arthur off. "Yeah. All right. Go already."

Arthur nodded, and started down the steps for his car.

Inside the courthouse, Fresnell and Larry Corning sat at a table in the basement cafeteria.

"You know what I like here?" said Fresnell. "The creamed corn. The rest of the food is garbage, but the creamed corn is really good." He looked up at Corning who was noisily chomping on a salad. French dressing ran down his chin. Corning seemed distracted.

"I have your signed statement saying you'd review it."

"Yeah, so?" said Fresnell.

"Well I drew up all the contracts," said Corning. "And I did all the work. I just wanted you to look it over."

"I did," said Fresnell brightly.

"For a seven thousand dollar fee?"

Fresnell shrugged. "In the statement you made me sign, it says, 'for a reasonable stipend.' There it is." The dressing ran on to Corning's tie. If there was one thing Fresnell hated, it was a sloppy eater.

"You call seven grand reasonable? Doctors treat each other for nothing. Where's some professional courtesy?"

It came to Fresnell suddenly that if Corning had only consumed his salad more neatly, he might have cut a couple of grand off the fee. Now, however, it was impossible. "Screw courtesy," he said. "This is business." He pushed his napkin in Corning's direction. "So what did you think when you heard about Porter?"

"Well, of course, it didn't surprise me," said Corning. "I knew when he punched me he was crazy."

"I thought that was a sign of sanity, myself," said Fresnell.

Corning did not smile. "Warren, seriously, about the fee, couldn't we discuss it . . . ?"

Three stories above, Ralph Agee sat at the defense table in Courtroom B. Alone. Behind the bench, Judge Burns leaned forward in his chair and motioned to the bailiff.

"What are we waiting for now?"

"Arthur Kirkland, Your Honor. Sentencing of Ralph Agee."

Burns slumped back. "Check the halls. See if he's lost."

"Yes, sir," said the bailiff. He hurried toward the back of the courtroom, as a puzzled and worried Ralph Agee looked around.

In the cafeteria, Corning was hacking at an ice-cream sundae; on the tip of his nose was a dot of hot fudge. "Make it fifty-five hundred," he was saying, "and we'll call it even."

141

Fresnell was beginning to tire of the game. He'd watched a ton of food disappear into Corning's voracious maw, another ton deposited on his face and clothing. The man was nauseating. Fresnell shook his head slowly, then glanced up at the clock. "Oh crap!" he said, slapping his forehead. "Arthur's case. I forgot Arthur's case." He stood up and pushed away from the table.

"Wait a minute," said Corning, packing in a final mouthful of maple walnut. "We're not finished with—"

But Fresnell was bolting toward the door, orange-striped sport jacket flying behind him. "Sue me!" he called back. He did not bother to wait for the elevator, instead raced up the three flights of stairs and hurried down the corridor. When, breathless, he finally entered Courtroom B, Judge Burns had given up.

"Okay," said Burns to the bailiff, "let's move on here."

Fresnell trotted forward down the center aisle. "Uh, Your Honor" he called. "Uh, just one moment, Your Honor." He crossed in front of the defense table, and steadied himself with one hand. He concentrated on not gasping. "I'm sorry I'm late, Your Honor, but Arthur Kirkland had an emergency, and I'm filling in."

Burns looked down, annoyed. "All right. Let's get on with this. I have a copy of Ralph Agee's probation report in front of me. Mr. Fresnell, are you familiar with this report?"

Fresnell, who hadn't had time to look at it, nodded. "Yes I am, Your Honor."

From the table behind him, Agee whispered, "Who are you?"

"Mr. Kirkland asked me to handle this for him."

"Who are you?"

"Don't worry. It's just a routine matter. You'll be out in a second."

Burns thumbed through the file. "Mr. Fresnell, is there anything you'd like to say about this report?"

Fresnell pulled the folder Arthur had given him from his attaché case. "No, Your Honor," he said, "I think it's all there in front of you."

"Well, I'm not satisfied," said Burns curtly.

"What?" said Fresnell. Something nagged at the back of his mind, something he couldn't remember.

"In view of what I see here," said Burns, "I sentence Ralph Agee to three years." He tapped his gavel on the bench and shut the folder.

Agee sat unmoving, looking at Fresnell. "What's happenin', man?" he asked as the guards approached him. One of the officers put his hand on Agee's shoulder. "Hey, I don't unnerstand. Hey, man, what's goin' down?"

Fresnell thumbed through the sheets in the folder, careful to avoid Agee's gaze.

The guards stood Agee up and led him slowly away. "Who *are* you?" he asked over his shoulder. "Who *are* you?" His voice was pitched with dawning panic. "Hey—" He disappeared out the side door.

At the back of the folder, Fresnell saw the yellow sheet.

At six in the evening he trudged slowly through the underground garage until he came to the gray Eldorado. It had been a tiring day, and he was hungry. In twenty minutes he would be home. Sandy had said there'd be lasagne for supper, and French onion soup —two of Fresnell's favorite dishes in all the world. He slowly eased the Cadillac out of the space and headed for the exit.

There was a squealing sound that suddenly grew louder. Fresnell thought it might be the water pump, perhaps a loose fan belt. He'd have to get it changed. He saw it from the corner of his eye, a subliminal blur that elongated into a car, careened in front of him, and spun halfway around so that it faced him broadside. Too late, he pounded the brake pedal as far as it would go. As if in an underwater ballet, the

Caddy kept moving dreamily forward, crashing slow-motion into the other vehicle and crunching into the left rear door. Fresnell sat in stunned rigidity as the other driver jumped from his car. He moved quickly toward the Caddy.

Fresnell had two immediate thoughts, curiously opposite in nature: It was a mistake to get into an accident with a lawyer—he would sue the balls off the guy; and on the other hand, the guy was running *toward* his car—perhaps this was a gangland execution, some former client, unhappy with his performance. The man was angrily pounding on the roof of the Caddy with his fists. Fresnell pictured deformed metal.

"Get out of the car!" yelled the man. "Get out of the car!"

Gingerly, not thinking clearly, Fresnell lowered the electric window just enough to let him peer upward. He stared in disbelief. It was Arthur. "What are you —crazy?" he said. His relief gradually became tinged with anger. The nerve. . . !

"Get out!" yelled Arthur.

"All right," said Fresnell, "just back away." He marveled at how irritated Arthur seemed; clearly, it was he who'd caused the accident. "What the hell's wrong with you?" he said.

"Out!"

Fresnell opened the door and got out. Immediately, he checked the roof, found several small depressions. "Look what you did. You dented my car."

"Tell me about it," said Arthur.

Fresnell looked at him uncomprehendingly.

"Tell me about Agee."

Finally, Fresnell understood, understood it all. Even so, he thought, he has no right. "It got by me," he said softly.

"It got by you?"

Fresnell looked at Arthur's face. He had seen that expression once before today . . . somewhere. . . .

He had it—Jay on the courthouse steps as they carried him out on the gurney.

Arthur swung his arm over Jay's shoulder. His fist came down on top of the Caddy.

Instinctively, Fresnell shoved him away. "Get off the car!"

"Agee didn't have to go to jail," said Arthur.

"Art, I told you, I admit it, I—"

"You understand that? Do you!"

"Art, you're really being unreasonable. . . ."

"He did *not* have to go to jail!"

Fresnell no longer was frightened. "So he gets out on parole in ten months. Listen, it's not all my fault. You *know* I don't like those penny-ante bullshit cases. I was doing you a favor."

"Favor!" said Arthur. "What kind of favor?"

Damn, thought Fresnell, first that slob Corning tries to wheedle me out of a fee, and now this maniac is all hot and bothered over a favor *I* did *him.* You can't win with people. They expect the impossible. "Nickel and dime!" he said. "It's all nickel and dime!"

Arthur shook his head. "Don't you care?" he said. "Don't you even care?"

Fresnell got back in his car. "Oh, spare me the pious bullshit. If you care so much, *you* should have been in the courtroom." He started the Caddy and backed it up several feet. "You're goddamn right I care. But not about them!"

"They're people!" Arthur shouted.

"They're not," said Fresnell through the window.

"They're just all people, Warren."

"If he's not in jail this week, he'll be in next. And that's the goddamn truth, Kirkland. You know it." He saw Arthur head toward the front of the car, and got out to follow him.

Arthur studied the Caddy for a moment, then aimed a powerful kick at the front grille.

"Hey!" said Fresnell.

"No, he won't be in jail next week!"

Fresnell inspected the grille. A small part of his mind was already calculating. This had to be seven hundred bucks at least, maybe eight hundred. He'd get an estimate for two thousand, bill Arthur fifteen hundred in the spirit of friendship. "Goddamn you!" he said. "Appeal it!"

"You don't understand. . . ."

"You know it's Probation's fault. Just get away from the car! Why are you making such a big deal over this? It's a mistake. Appeal."

Arthur's shoulders slumped, his fury finally spent. "I can't appeal it. He's dead. Half an hour after they put him in lock-up, he hanged himself."

The sense of the words seeped in slowly, and with them, awareness. Arthur was so upset because his client had killed himself. But, surely, Arthur couldn't control what went on in prison, or in the minds of convicts. Except this client didn't have to *be* in prison. This was an oversight. . . . "Jesus," said Fresnell softly. He felt his legs go weak and, for an instant, his vision blurred. The oversight was his, and a man had died because of it. He began to shake his head. "I'm sorry, Arthur. Jesus . . ."

"Yeah, well I . . . ," said Arthur. He walked back to his car.

Fresnell stood unmoving, craving now the most meager words of absolution from Arthur, words he would never get. "I'm really sorry, Art. Jesus. Really. I didn't mean . . ."

Arthur kicked the fender of his own car, then got in and started it. He disengaged the parking brake and headed slowly for the exit of the garage. In the rearview mirror he could see Fresnell, frozen in place next to his Eldorado, eyes staring, rigid as a slab of ice.

The next morning he went to see Jeff McCullaugh. Arthur had been awake most of the night, thinking, thinking about Ralph Agee and his final moments.

Had he already been attacked before he took the ultimate way out, or was his imagination sufficiently vivid to project what would happen to him? And how exactly had he hanged himself; did he use the laces from his shoes? A belt? A bedsheet torn into strips? Did he tie it to the light fixture? To the tops of the cell bars? What did he stand on? Was his cellmate there, and did he just watch? Did the blond wig fall off as Agee was strangling? And what did they do with it? Would he wear it in his coffin?

The questions would not stop, but kept reverberating in Arthur's head. In the morning, he knew he had to see McCullaugh. After a quick breakfast he drove to the State Penitentiary; the dark, heavy-stoned building loomed like a medieval fortress against the chilled gray of the sky.

Inside, he waited more than twenty minutes in the visitors' room before a guard finally emerged from somewhere and walked toward him. "Mr. Kirkland?"

Arthur stood up. A cold nausea began to work its way into his throat. First Agee, then . . .

"Mr. Kirkland, Jeff McCullaugh is sick today. He can't see you."

"What? Well, where is he?"

"Infirmary," said the guard.

"What happened?"

The guard shrugged. "Search me. Maybe he has a cold."

"Right," said Arthur. "Or maybe his fingernails needed cutting. Look, I'm his attorney. I'd like to see him."

The guard pursed his lips.

"I insist on it," said Arthur.

The guard looked over his head. Finally, he pointed. "You go out that door, make a right. Go down the end of the corridor, all the way till you can't go no more, then up the steps. Top of the steps make another right. They gotta put a special stamp on your visitor's pass, you stop at the desk."

Arthur nodded curtly. Ten minutes later he was in the hospital ward, looking down at a sleeping Jeff McCullaugh. McCullaugh had always been thin, but he now looked emaciated. The bones in his face stretched the mottled white skin seemingly to the breaking point. His blond hair was clumped and matted, and bruises were visible on his scalp.

"He looks . . . bad," said Arthur.

Next to him, the doctor shook his head. "No, no, most of it is surface stuff, nothing really serious. The first day there was some slight internal bleeding but that's cleared up now."

"I dunno," said Arthur, "I mean, his whole appearance . . ."

"A lot of the men lose weight at the beginning," said the doctor. "It's a big adjustment. The food's different, there's a lot of stress, but eventually they stabilize."

Men in the adjacent beds were sitting up and staring at them. Somehow, they looked to Arthur much healthier than McCullaugh.

"I would say," continued the doctor, "that he should be well enough in a day or so to be sent back to his cell."

McCullaugh moaned, stirred in his sleep.

I wonder what he's dreaming, Arthur thought. "Can't you keep him here a couple of weeks?" he asked.

"I don't see any reason for that."

"You don't?"

The doctor headed for the exit and Arthur followed. "Look," the doctor said, "I have sent a memo to the warden several times about this prisoner."

"He can't take these beatings much longer," said Arthur. "No one could."

The doctor stopped at the double door. "I know," he said, "that this man is a victim. I know he is not starting these fights. And believe me, I know what

148

conditions are like here—far better than you do, Mister, uh, Kirkland."

"Then that's all the more reason not to let this be on your conscience."

The doctor shrugged. "My conscience is perfectly clear, believe me, it is. I do what I can. In this particular case, all I can do is send memos. As a doctor I attend to these people medically—"

"And as a human being you can't shut your eyes," said Arthur.

"I try not to," said the doctor.

"Well try a little harder, all right?"

The doctor pushed open the doors. He raised his eyebrows. "What can I do? I'll send another memo."

The house was a white colonial situated on about an acre of lushly wooded land. No one was home. Damn! thought Arthur. It was impossible. He had made an appointment. The man wouldn't dare just ignore him. He walked tentatively along the side of the house on a path of red bricks, squeezed by some evergreens, went through a six-foot-tall slatted wooden gate . . . and saw the dome. It was made of some kind of plastic, translucent, slightly higher than the house, and almost as long. Arthur approached it cautiously, touched the smooth exterior, trod slowly around the periphery looking for an entrance. He found one near the center, a metal door sealed with soft rubber at the edge. He pushed against it, heard a faint hissing sound, pressed even harder as he met unexpected resistance. He squeezed inside, and the door shut behind him. Air pressure, he realized. Held up the dome and made the door hard to open.

It was humid. At first he thought it was a tennis court, then realized there wasn't enough height. Lobs would hit the ceiling. He saw now it was a swimming pool, a mammoth rectangle with underwater lights, two diving boards, surrounded by tables and chairs and chaise lounges. A man was swimming laps along the center. He wore racing goggles and a nose clip. Arthur walked parallel to him along the pool's edge.

"Judge Fleming?"

Fleming, giving no sign of having heard, executed a perfect racing turn at the far end of the pool. Arthur started to walk back. "Judge Fleming?"

"Fleming's head came out of the water and with it, his mouth. "Yes. How'd it go, Arthur?" He kept swimming, and Arthur kept walking.

There was something surreal in the quality of their voices, an echo effect produced by the dome, and that, together with the moist heat and diffused light made Arthur feel slightly woozy. He strained to maintain concentration. "I spoke to the DA's office about dropping the charges. Off the record they'd like to, but they're concerned about appearances. There's been a great deal of press."

Fleming submerged, stroked, and came up. "Who did you talk to?"

"Frank Bowers."

"Well, he's right. If we didn't go to court on this, it would look like a political maneuver."

"Those were exactly his feelings."

"I want it all out in the open. I'm very pleased, Arthur." Fleming reached the other end, kicked, somersaulted, rolled, and pushed off. It was a perfect turn.

Arthur reversed direction, abruptly sank into one of the chaise lounges. Damned if I'm going to chase that fucking shark all over the pool, he thought. Perspiring from the humidity, he opened his overcoat and waited until Fleming's head cleared the water. "Now back to McCullaugh," he yelled.

"What about him?"

"What's going on? This thing's been dragging on forever."

Fleming stroked and spoke from the edge of his mouth. "The groundwork's all set."

"Which means what?"

"He'll be out in no time."

"I've been telling him that for weeks," yelled Arthur. " 'No time' is taking forever."

"Tell him to be patient." Fleming's face sank below the surface, but Arthur could still see his ears.

"Patient! While you're taking your afternoon dip, an innocent kid is in prison, scared out of his mind and fighting for his life."

Fleming touched the far end of the pool, but instead of turning he reached up and hoisted himself out. He was wearing a tiny blue nylon stretch bikini. Even at the distance, Arthur could see the outlines of his genitalia. "Good!" said Fleming. "Prison should be a frightening place."

"You're not serious," said Arthur. "I'm not hearing this from a judge."

"Let those criminals create their own hellhole. Why should we help them once they're behind bars? Our job is to maintain law and order on the streets." Fleming grabbed a fluffy red towel and gently began to pat himself dry.

"All prisoners are not equal," said Arthur, but Fleming seemed not to hear.

"If someone chooses to violate the law, put him away where there is no law and see how long he lasts."

"There are men in prison for murder," said Arthur, "and there are men there because of a clerical error."

"In fact, take away the guards." Fleming nodded, pleased with the new idea. "Use them only to keep the prisoners in—not to protect them from themselves."

Fleming carelessly dropped his towel, the action of a man who had a housekeeper. He walked toward one of the diving boards. "If they want to kill each other, fine and dandy."

Arthur removed his overcoat as Fleming passed. "I think you're nuts," he said. "This is beyond a difference of opinion, I think you're absolutely off the wall."

Fleming, unperturbed, stood at the rear of the diving board. "Prison should be so vile and horrible that the place itself becomes a deterrent to crime." He took a trial run to the end of the board, bounced once, then sauntered back.

"The idea of punishment to fit the crime does not work. We need *unjust* punishment. Hang someone for armed robbery. Try it! We've got nothing to lose."

Fleming hesitated at the back of the board. "Do you understand what I'm saying to you, for God's sake?"

"Yes I do," said Arthur. "You don't think we should do anything for them at all. No rehabilitation, no nothing."

Fleming broke confidently toward the water. "The concept of rehabilitation is a farce." He bounced twice. "Do you honestly think that bringing Johnny Cash into prisons to sing railroad songs is going to rehabilitate anyone?" He soared high in the air, did one forward roll and a half-twist before entering the water, his body perfectly vertical. He knew the dive was excellent and he was glad, glad to impress the young snot who happened to be his lawyer. Let him see what discipline and execution were. Precise in the law and precise in his dives. Sleek as a seal, he swam underwater the length of the pool. What would the ultraliberal pinko have to say about *that?* he wondered as he broke the surface. He wiped the water from his eyes and pulled himself up over the side, then carefully looked around.

To his disappointment, the dome was empty.

12

ARTHUR ate lunch alone. He had gone to visit Jay right after leaving Fleming. Of course, it had been sad. Not so much seeing Jay—he was, in fact, much better—but hearing him talk so eagerly about coming back. It had been the mildest of nervous breakdowns (in psychiatric terms). He was suffering from classical psychotic depression. Textbook symptoms. Brain couldn't rid itself of a certain noxious chemical, and the normal neurotic funk turned into plate-throwing carnage. But it was on the wane now. Shock treatments wouldn't be necessary. Therapy with drugs, a bit of psychoanalysis, a little rest, and he'd be well on the way to recovery.

Which was why Arthur was sad. Recovery to *what?* he wondered. To more insanity? So he could argue cases before judges like Fleming and Rayford? So he could save the guilty and see the innocent sacrificed? It was better to stay insane. All right, Arthur realized, not better, but coming back was no bargain. He wondered what he was doing with his life—then paid the check, buttoned his overcoat, and stepped outside. Immediately, a Cadillac pulled up to the curb.

"Arthur," called Carl Bennett. "Get in."

Arthur could see a heavily made-up woman in the back. "Carl, is this another problem? Because—"

"No, no, everything's fine. Come on, get in."

Arthur crossed to the passenger side and slid in next to Bennett.

"Your partner's coming back, I hear," said Bennett.

"Yeah."

"They going to let him practice again?"

"Sure."

Bennett chuckled. "Who says you got to be sane to practice law, right?"

"Just the opposite," said Arthur. He was irritated that Bennett had interrupted his sulk. Were not resentment and bitterness among the most satisfying of human emotions? A vinegar bath for the psyche? "Come on, Carl," he said, "whaddaya want?"

"Got a little present for you," said Bennett, grinning.

Arthur looked at him questioningly. "It's not my birthday, Carl. What gives?"

"Nothing. You did me a favor; I'm doing you one, that's all. Give him the picture, sweetheart," Carl said to the floozy in the back seat.

Arthur took the manila envelope, opened it, and burst out laughing. "Holy shit," he said quietly. "Holy shit!"

Carl was grinning ear to ear. "What do you think? Does that take care of my legal fees for the next two years?" Carl knew he would not be forgotten for this one. It would set him up with Arthur for a long time.

Arthur continued staring at the five-by-seven glossy. There were three people in the photograph. William Zinoff, the head of the Ethics Committee, looked just darling in black mesh stockings, a pink garter belt and a matching padded bra. Seeing him dressed like that, all Arthur could think of was how flabbergasted Gail would be. That made him smile all the more. Zinoff was on the left side of the trio. Standing on the right was Judge Fleming. He was decked out in a black leather athletic support, which reminded Arthur of the very brief bathing trunks he had seen Fleming in at his house. The pièce de résistance, however, was the skin tight black leather vest, covered in front and back with shiny metal studs. Self-righteous, pompous ass, Arthur thought as he stared at the photo. Standing between Zinoff and Fleming was a young girl, no more than ten years old. She was naked and had her back to the camera. Her hands were tied behind her back and there were discolorations on her buttocks. She stared up at Fleming. Arthur was no longer grinning. There was nothing amusing about what he was looking at. Instead, he was feeling rage—disgust and anger!

"That filthy, lying pig," he murmured.

"Well there you have it. Judge Fleming and child," said Carl. He was still enjoying his moment of glory.

Arthur looked up and saw Bennett grinning. "Jesus," he said, "I don't believe this!"

Carl took Arthur's cue and donned a more serious expression.

"Where'd you get this?" asked Arthur.

"No, no. I can't tell you that. The guy I got this from keeps his own copies of things for personal enjoyment. Specializes in pictures of well-known people. I'm telling you, Art, you wouldn't believe the kinds of shots—entertainers, public officials, everything. Fleming is nothing. Years ago, this guy had a few shots of Marilyn Monroe that would have . . ."

Bennett put his hand on Arthur's arm. "Art," he said. "Take this for what it is. A gift. A gift out of thin air. A token of my appreciation."

Arthur slipped the picture back in the envelope, put the envelope in his jacket pocket.

Three days later, jury selection began for the Fleming trial. In the *voir dire* proceeding, prosecuting and defense attorneys were permitted to question prospective jurors and attempt to disqualify them for prejudices that might affect their judgment. In addition, each side could exercise six peremptory challenges, by which a juror was excused without specific grounds. Arthur's strategy was clear. As usual in a rape case, avoid women. As usual in a case involving a professional man, avoid people of lower economic status. Avoid people who might not respect the law or judges: young people, men with beads and long hair, provocatively dressed women. Of course, the prosecution's strategy would be exactly the reverse, and so the peremptory challenges had to be exercised with discretion, and the questioning sharply directed to elicit prejudices and dismissals for cause. By the third day, eleven jurors had been selected. Arthur had used four peremptory challenges, Bowers, three. The judge in the case was Rayford.

A woman was on the witness stand. She was in her thirties, pretty, neatly dressed in a brown suit. Bowers had already questioned her and made no challenge. Arthur paced carefully in front of the bench.

"Have you read about this case in the papers, Miss Stewart?"

"Yes."

"Have you formed an opinion about the guilt or innocence of the defendant?"

"No."

"Do you find it repellent that an older man would have sexual relations with a girl much younger than himself?"

"No." Faint smile.

"Do you find it strange that a man and woman might have sexual intercourse on the first date?"

"Not at all." Her eyes met Arthur's and lingered.

"Is there any activity between a man and a woman you would morally disapprove of?"

"Not really." Full smile.

"Even if someone got hurt?"

"I wouldn't want to see anyone get hurt. Unless they wanted to be, that is. As long as they got what they wanted . . ."

"Do you respect the law, Miss Stewart?"

"Yes."

"Do you respect those who administer it?"

"Yes. Generally."

Arthur looked at her carefully. His previous peremptories had all been women, but this one . . . She watched him with her eyes wide open. Sometimes, once in a while, a woman juror could be literally mesmerized by a male lawyer. Occasionally, it even happened to female witnesses. They lost the power of discrimination, concentrated not on the substance of an argument but on the tone of voice. They looked at your lips, your eyes, your crotch—he had seen it happen. Such a juror would be an invaluable ally. Probably, woman lawyers found the same thing with men, but Arthur had never seen it. He drew close to the witness stand, made his voice somewhat deeper and more throaty, though not enough to burlesque the situation. "Does the idea of sexual violence excite you?"

The woman's lips parted slightly. She swallowed. "I don't think so," she said, her voice slightly above a whisper.

"Would you consider yourself a sexually liberated woman?"

"Yes. Definitely."

Arthur turned away and walked back to the defense table. No sense going any further. The girl might just fling her arms around him and be rejected for cause. Fleming was sitting stiffly, but his lips had a half-grin. He had sensed what was going on. Arthur swiveled to face the bench.

"Your Honor, I find this woman acceptable. We have no objections."

"All right," said Judge Rayford. "That concludes jury selection. This trial will begin tomorrow at 10:00 A.M." He tapped the gavel.

Fleming rose from the defense table, stretched, and leaned over the rail of the spectator section. He whispered something to a man seated in the first row, and the two of them laughed aloud as Arthur watched coldly.

The call came at 7:00 P.M., just as Arthur was leaving. It was from the police: Could he please get over to the State Penitentiary as soon as possible. There was an emergency involving a client of his, a Mr. McCullaugh. They would send a car.

Arthur didn't wait. Twenty minutes later he pulled his BMW up to the penitentiary gate, and immediately got out. It was drizzling, and the blue revolving-beacon lights of a dozen police cars lent a strange underwater cast to the scene. Clusters of men stood talking and waiting; there were occasional pops of flashbulbs and newsmen spoke quietly into tape recorders. As his eyes became accustomed to the darkness, Arthur could see figures posted on the walls, uniformed men with rifles. He walked past a TV minicam crew where a man in civilian clothes was being interviewed by a woman reporter.

". . . fellow is holding two hostages in the hospital clinic," Arthur heard the man say. "So far as we know, the hostages have not been hurt." Arthur paused.

"Dr. Bayliss," said the reporter, "can your unit provide any psychological insights into the character of people who engage in this type of violence?"

Arthur began to move on.

"Yes. In the past few years we have begun to develop a behavorial profile based on the manner in which a person deals with his hostages."

Arthur found a policeman. "I'm Arthur Kirkland," he said. "McCullaugh's lawyer. I got a call asking me to come."

"Hold on," said the officer, "I'll get the captain." He disappeared behind the gate.

"For instance," the police psychologist was saying, "if the hostages' hands are tied behind them rather than in front, this indicates a more violent nature. If bags, or sacks, are placed over the hostages' heads, this would suggest a greater possibility of their eventually being killed. Mediation would be less likely."

"Dr. Bayliss," said the reporter, "in this case tonight, has there been any indication that you consider particularly ominous?"

A uniformed man called sharply from the entrance. "Arthur Kirkland?"

"Here," said Arthur. He was soaking wet from the rain.

The man held open the gate. "This way, please."

Arthur followed him into the building and they walked down a long hallway.

"Captain Oresky," said the man, offering his hand.

Arthur shook it.

"Happened about an hour and a half ago," said Oresky. "The clinic doctor felt he was well enough to be sent back to his cell. He was signing the release papers when . . . tell ya, no one knows exactly what happened." They turned a corner. "Boy, rainin' like a bitch out, huh? It was only drizzlin' before, but now it's coming down."

"Yeah," said Arthur. He'd skipped lunch and his stomach was churning from the excitement and lack of food.

"Anyway," continued Oresky, "all of a sudden, McCullaugh has the guard's gun. Tell ya, these corrections guys, I don't know where they come from, you know?"

"It's a problem," said Arthur.

"I mean no training, no education . . . and motivation? Forget it. There's half your problem right there."

They headed up a flight of stairs. "This is going to be taken care of, isn't it?" said Arthur. "I don't want anything drastic happening here."

"That depends on him," said Oresky. They came to a landing and opened the door to a narrow corridor. "We're doin' what we can," continued the captain. "We can't sit on this for long, though. Too many goddamn criminals in this building."

They came to the door that led to the ward. The doctor, two prison officials, and three sharpshooters stood just outside.

"I'm sorry," said the doctor, spying Arthur. "He had to go back."

"Yeah, he had to, huh?" said Arthur.

"I'm surprised he's even awake in there. I loaded him up on Thorazine just before he was supposed to leave."

Arthur moved past the men and opened the door. The room was pitch black except for one glaring bulb that shone harshly from an upturned gooseneck lamp on the floor. Arthur stood framed in the doorway, shielding his eyes. "Jeff?" he called tentatively.

"Hey, Mr. Kirkland!" said a voice at the other end of the room.

"Jeff, can I come down there?"

"Yeah, a little ways."

Arthur moved down the center aisle. The beds were all empty. Near the back of the room he could make out three shadow figures resting on the floor. Arthur sat down on one of the beds. "So . . . uh, what's new?" he asked.

McCullaugh laughed sluggishly. "You know, the usual."

Arthur waited. He felt extremely tired and rundown, a fatigue that surpassed the purely physical. He had no experience in these situations. He did not know the right things to say. Should've lingered to hear the police psychiatrist, he thought. He'd know. Should've lingered. McCullaugh remained silent. Arthur took a deep breath. "This is crazy, Jeff," he said finally.

"Yeah, I know," said McCullaugh. "And you wanna hear what's really crazy? I don't know what the hell I'm doing, or how any of this is supposed to work. Imagine, me taking hostages." He laughed nervously. "Christ, took me forty minutes to tie them up."

Arthur still couldn't see, but pictured McCullaugh

160

biting his nails. He heard something near the door, saw a uniformed figure crouched in the opening.

"Tell them not to come in here!" shouted McCullaugh quickly.

"Hey!" said Arthur to the guard. "Hey!"

"I don't want anybody in here!" yelled McCullaugh. His voice had a high-pitched urgency.

Arthur saw the guard back away.

"They're outside, you know," said McCullaugh. "They've got sharpshooters with those night viewscopes. They're posted all around."

"Jeff," said Arthur softly, "there's no way you can win this thing."

"You wanna hear something else?" said McCullaugh. "I don't know how to make a good knot. Knots are something I never learned. I mean, would you know how to do that?"

"What? Tie people up?" Arthur considered. It was a problem. The most elementary anti-social act required weeks of training. Normal people were simply not cut out for such work. "I don't know," he added. "I never thought about it. I guess you just make a . . . Jesus . . . a square knot, probably." He shook his head. "It's the easiest, I guess. I really don't know."

"Take a look, would you, Mr. Kirkland? See if I did it all right."

"You want me to look?"

"Yes."

Arthur stood up, hesitated, then walked slowly down the aisle of beds until he came to the rear wall. The hostages were seated behind a bed on the right, McCullaugh crouched in the corner. A handgun rested on McCullaugh's thigh. Arthur bent down near the two guards and tugged on the ropes that bound their wrists. They felt tight, but he still could barely see.

"Very good, Jeff," he said. "These are good knots." He stood and faced McCullaugh. "Jeff, this is their game. They gear up for this kind of number."

McCullaugh blinked and squeezed his face with his hand. "I understand," he said. "It's so hard to believe, me taking hostages. It's funny, it's really funny. And look at this." He held up the gun.

Instinctively, Arthur leaned backward.

"You're worried?" said McCullaugh. "It took me fifteen minutes to realize there was a safety catch on this thing." He yawned.

The Thorazine, thought Arthur. He must really be terrified to stay alert under that kind of medication. "Okay," he said, "so let's end it now, all right? I don't wanna be here; I'm cold, wet, hungry, and you don't wanna be here either—so let's end it, huh? I know you're tired of hearing this, but I swear to you, I'll have you out in no time."

There was silence.

"Jeff?"

The words, when they came, were strangled. "I can't stand anymore." There was a sound that might have been a moan. "They raped me. A bunch of times . . . and other things."

"Oh Christ," said Arthur.

"I can't take it. . . ."

Arthur began edging over on the bed. "Look, Jeff, I'm going to move a little closer to you. Okay? Is that okay?"

McCullaugh nodded, his face still in shadow.

"I don't know what to say," continued Arthur. "I know there isn't anything to say. But you've got to give up."

"Give up! To who? Who can I give up to? Everybody's screwed me, who else is there?"

Arthur nodded. "Look, I know how you feel—"

"You don't," said McCullaugh. "You really don't."

"You're right," said Arthur, "I don't. It doesn't matter. This can't work."

"Mr. Kirkland, go away, please." McCullaugh flipped the gun carelessly. "I just want to stay right here in this corner. That's all I want. Just this much free space."

"I swear to God, it'll be okay."

"God," echoed McCullaugh bitterly. "Who's he? I think they raped him, too."

"You have my promise, Jeff—"

"You did what you could," said McCullaugh. "I'm not blaming you. But nothing makes sense anymore. Nothing."

Arthur leaned back. He was out of ideas. There was nothing sensible left to say. "So what are you going to do?" he asked after a while.

"Nothing!" shouted McCullaugh. "I don't want to do anything!"

"That's—you can't just sit there!" Arthur shouted back, exasperated more with his own lack of inventiveness than with McCullaugh's failure to act.

"Yes!" said McCullaugh. "I can."

"You can't."

"That's just what I want. I just want to sit here and be left alone."

Arthur shook his head. The two hostages, though not gagged, sat in absolute silence. Even their breathing was quiet. Five minutes went by. McCullaugh began to rub his legs. "Jesus," he said, "I'm stiff as a board."

"I'm not surprised," said Arthur. "Squatting like that is no good for your circulation.

McCullaugh slowly hauled himself up, using the bed for support. "Oh, man," he grunted, "I can hardly move. I think my foot fell asleep." He took a tentative step. "I hope I don't fall over." At that moment his upper body was outlined in the window frame. Three seconds later there was a sharp crack, a flat shattering of glass, and the top half of McCullaugh's head was simply blown away from the rest of him. It happened fast, no slow-motion, chiaroscuro fly-away of hair and blood and bone, just, *splat!* a melon hacked in two by a machete. An instantaneous cessation of existence. Dead before he fell.

The gurgle in Arthur's throat quickly became a ululating scream. And he was still screaming when they got to him.

13

MOST of the night he sat in his car. He did not care much for bars—the atmosphere of besotted criers-in-their-beer sitting around feeling sorry for themselves (and half the time being rolled after closing hour) did not hold much appeal. He was not religious, and so that excluded the churches. Besides, the idea of praying to any deity who had countenanced the event of that evening seemed fatuous, if not obscene. The all-night movies were unendurable and peopled by aggressive homosexuals. So Arthur sat in his car. The rain had tapered to a damp mist. The street lights were haloed.

During the hours driving back from the prison and sitting parked at the curb, one thing had helped him retain his sanity, one isolated, undeniable handgrip on the greased vertical pipe to madness: It was over. In that first millionth of a second that the bullet had entered his brain, Jeff McCullaugh was dead. Clinically, irretrievably dead. No cleverness, no heroic act, no complex strategy, however perfect, could salvage the situation. Recrimination, even self-recrimination, was pointless. It could not change the fact. Death was a product that could not be recalled, a sentence without possibility of appeal. And therefore, whatever was said, was done, was thought had to do only for the living, was for their trivial benefit and mental adjustment. The *fait accompli* stood.

At 3:45 A.M. Arthur drove to an apartment house on Preston Street. He walked to a phone booth on the corner, dialed, and waited. A sleepy voice answered on the fifth ring.

"Hello?" Her voice was slurred.

"Gail?"

"Who—Arthur? Arthur, is that you?"

"Gail, I'm sorry to wake you up. I'm really sorry."

"Where are you? Are you home?"

"I'm downstairs. I'll be in the lobby. Can you come down?"

"Yeah, I can. I—are you okay, Arthur? You sound . . ."

"Yeah, yeah, I'm fine. I'll see you in the lobby." He hung up.

The clock in the hall read 4:00 A.M. when she stepped out of the elevator. She was dressed in a beige coat and flat shoes and wore no makeup. Arthur kissed her lightly on the lips.

"Why didn't you come up?" she asked.

"I don't want to sit anymore," said Arthur. "I'm too nervous."

"I heard about McCullaugh," said Gail.

"You heard?"

"It was on TV. I'm sorry."

Arthur ignored her. From his pocket, he pulled out a small Manila envelope and handed it to her wordlessly. She opened it and withdrew the picture. He watched her lips part and her eyes widen.

"Ladies and gentlemen!" he said. "In the center ring—The Honorable Judge Henry T. Fleming, performing without the aid of a net. Ta-da!"

"I don't—Jesus!"

"Come on," said Arthur, "let's get some air."

They walked for many blocks, their footsteps resonating dully through the damp night. The chill, which had bothered Arthur early in the evening, was gone. Though he had not eaten, his hunger had vanished. He felt numb, an out-of-body sort of detachment, as though he was observing himself from a great height.

"Are you sure the photograph is real?" said Gail after a while.

"Yeah. I'm working for a pervert."

"I guess . . . I guess you weren't prepared for this."

"I don't know what to do," said Arthur. He didn't know what he expected. If there was one thing he had learned, it was that no one knew more about him than he did. Help, if it existed, would come from inside, not externally.

"Arthur," said Gail, "this photograph is disgusting, but it doesn't mean that Fleming raped Leah Shepard. It does not constitute proof."

"Come on," said Arthur, "the son-of-a-bitch is guilty."

"Then drop the case."

Arthur chuckled mirthlessly. "It's not that easy."

"Why not?"

Arthur wriggled the Manila envelope, now back in his coat pocket. "Because the head of the Ethics Committee—your boss—is blackmailing me."

"That's ridiculous."

"It's the truth. I work for a pervert and you work for a blackmailer."

"Blackmail! What for?"

Arthur shook his head. "I can't tell you." They came to a curb. Arthur took her hand as they stepped off.

"You don't trust me?" said Gail.

"That's right."

"Then why wake me up in the middle of the night? Why show me the picture?"

Arthur stopped. "Because . . . there's no one else to tell. No one. Believe me, if I could find one other person to turn to, I would."

They resumed walking. "Are you cold?" he asked after five minutes.

"No." She paused. "All right, yes. A little."

He put his arm around her.

"I think I know what it's about," said Gail.

"Yes? Tell me."

"After your session with the committee, we did a check on you."

Arthur squinted. "Wait a minute. This was going on while we were seeing each other?"

"Yes."

The numbness was gone. Arthur felt the juices of rage boil in his brain.

"There was some question," continued Gail, "as to whether or not you should be disbarred."

They passed a cop standing in a doorway; he was twirling a nightstick. "You mean to tell me," said Arthur, "that while we were sleeping together, you and the 'fellas' were making decisions on my *life?* My *life?*"

Gail looked at him. "Please . . . just let me finish. While we were in the midst of that, Mr. Zinoff stepped in and pulled your file. Said he wanted to review your case personally."

In the distance, Arthur saw the sky beginning to lighten. "They're tied in," he said absently. "Fleming, Zinoff, all tied in."

"That was the last we heard of it," said Gail. She clutched at his sleeve. "Arthur, I had no idea."

"Jesus, I— The whole thing stinks. Top to bottom. Only there is no bottom, it's endless."

"Then *do* something," implored Gail.

"What?"

"Go up against Fleming and take the consequences."

A cab sped by and whooshed through a curbside puddle, splashing Arthur's trousers with muddy water. He was too tired even to curse. "You know," said Arthur after another two blocks, "the only thing I know how to be is a lawyer. It's the only thing I'm good at. I'm beginning to think it's a skill not relevant to survival. I feel like a giraffe who finds himself suddenly surrounded by a hundred crocodiles. I mean, what the hell good, then, is the ability to eat off trees?"

"I'm sorry it's come to this," said Gail. "Believe me."

"I believe you," said Arthur. "I am too. For many reasons, not all of which have to do with pie-in-the-sky idealism, either. In addition to eating and paying the rent with the money I make, I support an ex-wife, and keep a little old man from dying in some state institution. A third of my clients don't have a dime, so I don't bother to collect a fee. My ready reserve account is not ready, and there is nothing in reserve; not a dime. My last act in practicing law would be to file for my own bankruptcy."

They were in a commercial district of small stores and restaurants. Street lamps and neon signs began to go off as the sky continued to brighten.

"It doesn't have to be that way," said Gail.

"No?"

"Look at the other side. The Ethics Committee is off your back and you'll win the Fleming case. You couldn't be in a better position."

"It doesn't bother you that a judge is guilty of raping a girl?"

"Wait a minute. You're making an assumption he's guilty because you hate him so much."

"I hate him, yes, but he *is* guilty."

"And, if so? It's still not your job to prosecute. As you of all people must know—a defense lawyer has to defend even those clients who are guilty."

Arthur was not in the mood for aphorisms. He wanted—what?—perhaps only sympathy, or support, even intelligent disagreement, and instead he got apothegms, bromides. "You don't understand, do you?" he said.

"I understand," said Gail. "I just don't agree."

Arthur stopped. Sooner or later, it had to come. Yet another in Arthur Kirkland's many moments of truth. The question could no longer be contained. "I just want to know one thing," he said. The sky was a gray slab. "If the committee had voted on my disbarment, which way would you have gone?"

Gail looked up at him, sensing the importance of her answer. Arthur, she knew, could not be fooled. "You violated the Code of Ethics," she said finally. "I would have voted 'Yes.'"

Arthur remained motionless. Only the expression in his eyes changed. A shutter, cutting them off.

"I'm sorry," said Gail softly. Her voice broke. "I wish I could lie to you."

Arthur touched her cheek with his fingers, lingered a final moment. Then abruptly he pivoted and slowly walked away. Gail watched him recede in the distance. What did he expect me to say? she wondered. *What did he expect?*

Arthur was at the retirement home by 8:00 A.M. He found Sam and Arnie in the recreation room sitting on aluminum chairs. Arnie was reading a newspaper, using a magnifying glass to enlarge the print.

"Big day today, huh?" said Arnie, when he saw Arthur. "I bet you're excited!"

"Yeah, a little. How'd you—"

Arnie held up the paper. FLEMING TRIAL BEGINS TODAY, the headline read.

Arthur looked over at Sam who seemed just to be becoming aware of him. "Grandpa?"

"He's a little under the weather today," said Arnie.

Sam smiled in recognition. "So, you're finally home on leave, huh?" He turned to Arnie. "Arthur's in the Coast Guard."

"I don't understand," mumbled Arthur. "It's getting worse."

"It depends," said Arnie. "He comes, he goes."

"Doesn't he remember anything?"

"He remembers everything! He just has trouble with the present."

Sam said something inaudible and then sat silently staring into space. Every once in a while his jaws worked spasmodically, and his left hand rippled with uncontrollable tremors.

"You didn't come for three weeks," said Arnie. "He missed you very much."

Arthur felt a sudden despair, what if his grandfather never recognized him again? What if he was . . . irreclaimable? "Well," he stammered, "I . . . I was very busy . . . uh, you know, getting ready. I had to, uh, get ready." The words echoed with unbearable triteness.

"I know, I know," said Arnie. He seized Arthur's arm in a gnarled hand. "It's very important for you. But you didn't come for three Tuesdays. He lost his sense of time."

Arthur looked over at Sam, who maintained his vacant stare. A stroke, perhaps, thought Arthur. Blackout in the brain. "You know, Arnie, I don't know what I'll do if he goes." Arthur swallowed hard, trying to choke down the balloon that swelled in his chest and throat. "He's the only real family I have." He shut his eyes tightly. "I'm a lawyer because of him. He wanted it for me and he made sure I got it. The day I passed the bar, he was the . . . happiest man. The happiest." He realized that both his cheeks were wet, and he turned his face so Arnie wouldn't see. "To him," Arthur whispered, "being a lawyer was the finest thing you could be."

His shoulders shook now, and even his fingers covering his face could not hide the eruption of tears. He was crying for the first time in a long time, crying for many reasons. In part the tears were for his clients, Agee and McCullaugh, in part for Gail, in part because he'd had no sleep and was exhausted, and in part for Sam, who barely knew who he was. But, after a while, when the crying would not stop, when the sobbing lasted longer than even the trying circumstances made reasonable, Arthur understood that most of all he was weeping for the foolishness of an old man's misplaced dream, and its embodiment—himself.

He spotted Fleming at the other end of the courthouse cafeteria. He was sitting at a table with two men, digging enthusiastically into a large plate of food. Arthur made his way through the milling breakfast crowd until he finally drew alongside Fleming's chair.

"See you a minute?" he said casually.

Fleming looked up, momentarily startled. "Oh, Arthur. Certainly." He turned back to the two men sitting with him. "Gentlemen, do you mind?"

The men, both wearing business suits, picked up their coffee cups and moved three tables away.

"I'm the only one who eats breakfast around here," said Fleming, spearing some home-fried potatoes. "Everyone else drinks coffee and gets fat. I eat like a pig and stay in perfect shape."

Arthur sat down. Nonchalantly, he opened his briefcase, removed the photo of Fleming, and nudged it over toward the judge's tray. Fleming looked at it casually.

"Where'd you get that?" he asked coolly. He swallowed a forkful of scrambled eggs.

"I've been carrying it for a couple of days."

Fleming sipped some coffee. "You know, the rest of the meals here are junk, but I'll tell you, you can't beat the breakfasts. They must have a different cook or something."

"I'd like to know what it means," said Arthur.

"Ah. What it means. I see the wheels spinning. Sex crime. Sex photo. Is he guilty?"

"Is he?"

Fleming chewed on a toasted English muffin. He watched Arthur intently, then grinned. "Yes. Are you surprised?"

"What about the polygraph and the witness?"

"Those were taken care of for me." He scooped up some more potatoes. "I can't believe these home fries. I may have to get another portion." He returned Arthur's stare without wavering. "Well, now you have it. Happy?"

"Yes," said Arthur, meaning it in a perverse way. The situation had at last been purified; no ambiguity remained. "You've made me very happy." He snatched the photograph from the table and stood up.

"See you in court," called Fleming cheerily.

14

RAYFORD sat at his desk admiring the sheen on the shotgun. The barrel gleamed dully in the dim glow of a 60-watt floor lamp. These endeavors took time, he knew, couldn't be rushed. The polishing job had consumed nearly a half-hour of concentrated effort. But it was important to get it right, to maintain in all things, a certain class. That had been the heroine's main concern in the last novel he had read, *The Heart Crumbles*. At the end, the principal character, trapped in a loveless marriage to an ogre of a husband, and also stricken with a slow but fatal disease, had managed to take her own life using a sewing machine. Rayford had found the ending quite moving. He snapped the shotgun open now, and placed two cartridges in the chambers. He pushed the chair away from the edge of his desk, closed the gun, and carefully placed the barrel between his legs. He opened his mouth and bit down on the other end. Good-bye, he thought. Good-bye, everyone. As for me, I move on. He inhaled deeply, shut his eyes, and reached for the trigger.

He couldn't find it. His hands groped futilely along the barrel. His fingertips searched frantically for the little projection. No use. He opened his eyes. So be it, he thought. He leaned down. Unfortunately, although of greater-than-average height, he had short arms. Always, it had been a problem in buying shirts (often, he had to make a cuff on the sleeves), and now it was a problem in committing suicide. His reach was a quarter-inch short of the trigger. This particular method of dispatch was simply not suitable for short-armed people. He began to gag on the barrel. He reached and gagged, reached again and gagged. The reach became a desperate lunge, the gag escalated to a retch. The geometry of the situation was defeating him. String, he realized finally. String was the solution. Necessity was the mother of invention.

There was a knock on the door. Rayford removed the shotgun from his knees and mouth, and placed it under the desk. He wiped his eyes, which had been tearing. "Yes?" he said easily.

A bailiff leaned in. "Your Honor, court's about to begin."

"Thank you," said Rayford.

The bailiff closed the door. Rayford crossed to a mirror and arranged his robe. Damn, he thought. These days a man hardly had any free time.

The courtroom was packed with hordes of the curious, relatives, friends, enemies, reporters—the usual crew who come to witness the spectacle. The media had worked the people into a frenzy of expectation. At the prosecutor's table, Frank Bowers spoke in low tones to a slight, pretty girl with sharp features—Leah Shepard. Across the room, Fleming leaned back in a chair at the defense table, while Arthur stood nearby, removing files from his briefcase. The stacks of folders arrayed neatly in front of him, he sat down. Fleming leaned over.

"You notice her?"

"Who?"

"Leah Shepard."

"Yeah," said Arthur.

"You must admit she's an attractive girl. I wouldn't mind seeing her again sometime."

Disgusted, Arthur turned away as the bailiff began to speak. "Hear ye, hear ye. The Criminal Court of Baltimore is now in session. All rise. The Honorable Francis W. Rayford presiding."

Everyone stood up. Rayford entered briskly and took his seat at the bench. He tapped his gavel. "The case before us is the State of Maryland versus Henry T. Fleming. The charges have been enumerated and explained at the last session." He faced the prosecutor. "Mr. Bowers, does the prosecution wish to make an opening statement?"

"Yes, Your Honor, we do," said the prosecuting attorney.

Bowers stood up, walked to the jury box, and began to speak. His statements were short, direct, uninspired—the false air of confidence of good representation. The prosecution would produce medical evidence that proved Leah Shepard had been raped, beaten, and sodomized. It would be shown that the defendant was with her during the time these events occurred. The victim herself would testify against the defendant. Whether the case was so open and shut or not, really didn't matter. Just make the jury think it is. Bowers was in good form today. Arthur was impressed.

Bowers sat down. The jurors' faces were impassive.

"The prosecutor," said Rayford, "has completed his opening statement." He turned toward Arthur. "Mr. Kirkland, are you ready."

Arthur rose. "Yes, Your Honor."

He walked across the room, glancing at Leah

174

Shepard as he did so. By a tactic known as *calling for the rule* on witnesses he could have had her excluded from the courtroom, but he had chosen not to. Fleming had concurred. Better to show them she's none the worse for wear, he had said, than let their imaginations run wild. Arthur rested his hands on the rail in front of the jury box. Bowers, of course, had been right to be low-key. Any hint that he was exploiting the sensational aspects of the case and the jurors' sympathies would lean toward the defendant.

"Your Honor," began Arthur, "Mr. Foreman, ladies and gentlemen of the jury. My name is Arthur Kirkland and I am the defense counsel for the defendant, Henry T. Fleming." He glanced briefly at the defense table. The image of his client's uncut toenails lingered distressingly in his mind. "Now, I'm saying Henry T. Fleming, because if I say *Judge* Henry T. Fleming, then I get angry. And a little embarrassed. Aren't you a little embarrassed? I mean, he's a judge."

Arthur pointed theatrically to Bowers. "Now *that* man, the prosecuting attorney, he couldn't be happier. He's a happy man today. He's going after a judge. And if he gets him, he's going to be a star. He's going to be the centerfold in this year's *Law Review*."

There were chuckles from the audience. Standard operating procedure, Arthur knew. The defense attorney played the crowd, hoping to carry the jury along in the general swell of personal approval. In a close case, it sometimes made the difference between acquittal or conviction. "To win this case," continued Arthur, "he needs your help, because you're all he has. He's counting on tapping that emotional reaction that says, 'Let's get somebody in power.'" He grinned. "Let's face it, we're all skeptical of those in power. We've all been burned."

We, thought Arthur. Not used cynically this time, not used only for a false sense of identification. In this *we,* he was out in front. "But what is the purpose of these proceedings?" he went on. "To see that justice prevails. And I'm sure that every reasonable person would agree that justice is the finding of truth. Now one truth, a tragic one, is that a young girl has been brutally raped. Another truth is that the prosecution"—carefully, he began to raise his voice—"does not have one witness, not one substantiating piece of evidence other than the testimony of the victim herself." His voice was thundering now, booming off the courtroom walls. "And yet another truth is that the prosecution is well aware that Henry T. Fleming voluntarily took a lie detector test and passed it! *He* told the truth!" shouted Arthur.

Immediately, Bowers sprang to his feet. "Objection, Your Honor! That's inadmissible evidence!"

Arthur touched a hand to his forehead, a gesture indicating he'd been carried away. "That's inadmissible evidence, and pretend I didn't say it. Ladies and gentlemen of the jury, I beg your indulgence. Disregard that remark." The old technique. Say it, and then take it back. Of course, it fooled no one, but so what?

"Mr. Kirkland!" said Rayford. "You're way out of line."

"I apologize, Your Honor."

"The jury is to disregard that remark," said Rayford. "Polygraph tests have not been proven 100 percent reliable, and are therefore inadmissible in a court of law. All right, proceed, Mr. Kirkland."

Arthur nodded. "What is the intention of justice? To see that the guilty are punished and the innocent are free. But it isn't as simple as that. Did you know that 90 percent of the people a defense attorney represents are guilty? Did you know that?" He paused to let the significance of the statement sink in. "Interesting, isn't it? Ninety percent. So that means when we fight to win a case, we are fighting to put a lot of guilty people back out on the streets as soon as possible. Where is the justice in that?"

He watched the jurors' faces, saw the looks of creeping uncertainty. They were beginning now to wonder. Something about this opening statement was not quite right. Nothing overt yet or obvious, just a hair too sprawling, philosophical . . . "Well, you see, it is the duty of the defense lawyer to uphold the rights of the individual . . . and it's the prosecution's job to see that the laws of society are upheld." He shook his head. "But we have a problem. Both men want to win. Regardless of the truth, regardless of justice." He felt his muscles tense, his breathing quicken. "Winning becomes all. So you see, it's just a game. And I intend to win this one." The jurors were now looking at him strangely. He felt the blood roaring in his neck and ears. His breath came in gasps. "The prosecution is not going to get this man . . ."—he turned toward Fleming, just as his voice broke—"because I am."

He saw Fleming suddenly stiffen. "My client," said Arthur, "the Honorable Henry T. Fleming, should go right to fuckin' jail. The son of a bitch is guilty!" He felt an immense, immediate relief. The fever had broken.

In the courtroom, there was stunned silence. "Mr. Kirkland . . ." Rayford said finally. "You're—"

"The man is slime!" shouted Arthur. He pointed an accusing finger at Fleming. His words were enunciated perfectly. "He is slime! If this man is allowed to go free, something very wrong is going on here."

That did it. From shocked quiet, the courtroom erupted into pandemonium. People applauded and yelled, booed and shouted, reporters ran into the aisle.

"Mr. Kirkland!" shouted Rayford. "You are out of order!" He banged the gavel repeatedly, without effect.

"This trial is a show!" continued Arthur. "That man"—Fleming was standing now—"that depraved, crazy man raped this girl here." He turned to Leah Shepard, addressed her personally. "And he'd like to do it again! He told me that!"

"Bailiff!" shouted Rayford over the din. "Remove the jury!" He turned to the court officers. "Clear the courtroom. C'mon, get them out of here."

The courtroom was filled with milling, excited people. Members of the press corps were hanging over the spectator railing.

"It's all coming apart!" yelled Arthur. "It's just a show. It's 'Let's Make A Deal'!" He strode to the prosecutor's table and leaned over a speechless Frank Bowers. "You wanna make a deal? C'mon, Frank. I've got one insane judge who likes to beat the shit out of girls. What do you want to give me? Three weeks probation?"

The courtroom was in total chaos. Rayford's gavel was banging steadily, but no one paid attention. "Shut that man up!" he yelled. "Officers! Forget those people! Get him out of here!"

Two officers moved toward Arthur, who had whirled to face Fleming for the last time. "You're supposed to stand for something, you son of a bitch. You're supposed to protect people, and instead you fuck and murder them!"

The officers reached out to grab him, but Arthur held up his palms. "Hold it! Hold it! Okay, okay. . . . I have completed my opening statement!" He smiled pleasantly, turned, and walked out of the courtroom.

The hall was jammed with reporters and photographers. As he pushed his way through, some held microphones to his mouth and others shouted questions, but Arthur said nothing. It was not until he had reached the courthouse lobby that he finally turned to address the crush of trailing members of the press. "Listen," he said, "I've got a lot more to say, but not right now, okay?" The crowd moaned. He was halfway out of the building when, grinning, he stopped again and reached into his jacket pocket. He handed the photo of Fleming and the young girl to the nearest reporter. "This should hold you for a while," he said. As everyone pushed in, trying to get a look, Arthur headed down the stone steps.

The day had finally cleared. It was cold but sunny. The sky was a bright blue, with a few fleecy cirrus clouds. Done, thought Arthur. For better or worse, done. Perhaps there would be no legal effect, perhaps even a negative one. Fleming's next lawyer would certainly ask for a new trial, a change of venue. The publicity, he would argue, now made a fair trial impossible. Eventually, Fleming might even get off. But he was ruined, thought Arthur. The photo would guarantee that he would never sit on the bench again. And as for himself . . . who knew? Life took peculiar turns. It was slippery and unpredictable, which was why, finally, it was tolerable.

A figure came up the steps toward him. It was a man, Arthur saw, dark-haired, neatly dressed, carrying an attaché case. Arthur looked away, then quickly back, squinted. The brown hair . . . "Jay?" he called tentatively.

The man passed him casually, reached up, and tipped his dark wig as if it were a hat. Underneath, his head was completely bald. "Good day," said Jay cordially. And then, as though nothing had happened, he continued up the steps.

Bestsellers from BALLANTINE

The best
in modern fiction from
BALLANTINE